ULTIMATE ENDING

BOOK 6

THE
STRANGE PHYSICS
OF THE
HEIDELBERG LABORATORY

Check out the full

ULTIMATE ENDING BOOKS

Series:

TREASURES OF THE FORGOTTEN CITY

THE HOUSE ON HOLLOW HILL

THE SHIP AT THE EDGE OF TIME

ENIGMA AT THE GREENSBORO ZOO

THE SECRET OF THE AURORA HOTEL

THE STRANGE PHYSICS OF THE HEIDELBERG LABORATORY

THE TOWER OF NEVER THERE

Cover design by Milan Jaram www.MilanJaram.com

Internal artwork by Jaime Buckley www.jaimebuckley.com

Reactor Core artwork by Radeartos

Enjoyed this book? Please take the time to leave a review on Amazon.

Dedicated to Lucas.
May you have many adventures to choose!

Welcome to **Ultimate Ending,**
where YOU choose the story!

That's right – everything that happens in this book is a result of
decisions YOU make. So choose wisely!

But also be careful. Throughout this book you'll find tricks and traps,
trials and tribulations! Most you can avoid with common sense and a
logical approach to problem solving. Others will require a little bit of luck.
Having a coin handy, or a pair of dice, will make your adventure even more
fun. So grab em' if you got em'!

Along the way you'll also find tips, clues, and even items that can help
you in your quest. You'll meet people. Pick stuff up. Taking note of these
things is often important, so while you're gathering your courage, you
might also want to grab yourself a pencil and a sheet of paper.

Keep in mind, there are *many* ways to end the story. Some conclusions
are good... some not so good.
Some of them are even great!
But remember:

There is only *ONE*

ULTIMATE
ENDING!

Welcome to the Heidelberg Physics Laboratory!

You are JEREMY HELLER, a recent graduate from the prestigious University of Zurich, where you received a Masters Degree in particle physics. You've got your first real job working at the Heidelberg Physics Laboratory, high in the Swiss Alps. Everyone from your university applied for the position, but you were the only one to be accepted. You can't believe how lucky you are!

You've only been working there a week, but already the laboratory is full of excitement. Built deep within the mountain is a particle accelerator, a long oval-shaped track that shoots atoms around and around *really* fast. The atoms are smashed into other atoms close to the speed of light, and the laboratory measures the pieces that come out. Cool!

Today is an especially important day. After months of testing, the physicists at the laboratory are smashing atoms together in a way that they hope will reveal a new sub-atomic particle: the Causality Neutrino. It would be the greatest physics discovery in the past century. And you might be a part of it!

You're all ready to get to work. You're wearing your white lab coat over dress clothes, and are riding the gondola all the way to the top of the mountain. From there you will need to take an elevator deep underground. Building the laboratory deep within the mountain ensures that the equipment is shielded by thousands of meters of rock, in case anything goes wrong. Although that seems highly unlikely-the physicists there are the best in the world!

You step off the gondola onto the mountain peak. The wind whips your lab coat all around, and the air feels like a thousand tiny needles on your face. The elevator is directly in front of you. Better get inside!

8

You hear the distant sound of machinery slowly grinding to life. The elevator is beginning to make its journey all the way to the surface. The wind is especially chilling this day, and already you can feel your black hair freezing to your head. Instead of wearing your nicest clothes for the demonstration, maybe you should have dressed warmer!

There's a muted *ding* as the elevator car arrives. The doors open slowly, and you jump through before they've barely opened. You press your shoulder against the wall of the car, trying to stay as far from the door as possible.

There are only two buttons: 'S' for Surface, and 'L' for Laboratory. You punch the 'L' with frozen fingers and the button glows yellow.

"Hey, wait!" drifts a voice from outside.

Did you imagine it? You lean your head sideways to take a look. The gondola station is a hundred feet away, and a new car has just come to a stop, rocking slightly on its cable. The door opens and a stream of people come pouring out, huddled in dark clothes.

One of them waves. "Hold the elevator!" It sounds like a girl.

Suffering the cold, you obediently stick your hand out to keep the doors from closing.

The people come jogging up the path and into the elevator. The person who waved is a girl, about your age, bundled head to toe in thick clothes. Straight black hair sticks out from underneath a woven cap and runs down her back.

"Thank you!" she says, out of breath. Her cheeks are flushed from the cold. "It would have been miserable waiting for the elevator car to go down and up again. I wish they'd build a waiting area shielded from the cold!"

You frown. She doesn't look like she works at the laboratory. "What are you doing here?" you blurt out.

The girl laughs. "That's not very polite." You begin to apologize, but she holds up a hand and says, "I'm teasing, I'm teasing. I'm here today for the demonstration. My father is Doctor Kessler."

You stare at the girl, awestruck. "Your father is Doctor Kessler?"

She gives a big nod. "Uh huh. So you'd better be nice to me, or I can get you in trouble."

You lick your lips out of nervousness. Kessler is the head physicist at the laboratory, in charge of the entire particle accelerator! If he finds out you were rude to his daughter...

The girl lets out a stream of giggles. "I'm just teasing you again. I wouldn't get you in trouble. You lab guys are easy to fluster." She sticks out a gloved hand. "Nice to meet you, Heller. I'm Penny. Penny Kessler."

Her glove is cold as you shake it. "How'd you know my name?"

Her face grows serious. "Dad was complaining last night about one of the interns. I assumed it was you. Looks like I was right, huh?"

Your mouth hangs open, horrified.

Penny's face is suddenly split by a wicked grin. "Okay, you've got me again. My dad's never mentioned you. I knew your name because it's on your name tag, silly." She points.

You look down at your coat breast, where a plastic clip-on tag says: J. HELLER. "Are you always this cruel to people you've just met?"

She flashes a white smile. "Just being friendly! So what's the 'J' stand for?"

You tell her.

"Nice to meet ya, Jeremy. Hey–no more joking around." She points to the path, where the other four men from the gondola are approaching the elevator. "Those are investors from the city. They're here to see the demo. If it doesn't go well, dad says they're going to pull their funding."

Uh oh. You had heard rumors that the investors weren't happy, but had assumed they weren't true.

The four men pile into the elevator. They're each wearing dark coats which drape to their ankles, with full suits underneath. One of them frowns at you. "Vat are ve vaiting for" he asks in a German accent.

You realize your hand is still holding the car. "Oh, sorry," you say, removing it. The man nods to himself.

The doors close.

10

The elevator makes its slow descent into the mountain. As you do every time, you wonder how a single elevator could travel so far. The laboratory must be at least a kilometer underground. Your ears pop, so you move your jaw around to unclog your ears, like you're on an airplane. About a minute later you have to do it again.

Finally the hum of the elevator reaches a lower pitch as you slow down, and then stop completely.

The doors open.

The entrance room to the Heidelberg Physics Laboratory feels like the lair of a James Bond villain: the side walls are carved rock, making it obvious you are deep inside a mountain, and the air has a cool, drafty feel. The wall directly opposite you has a single, massive door in the center. It's five meters tall and three wide, and covered with blinking lights and electronics. It's made of dull metal, and you know it can withstand a nuclear explosion, if need be.

The room is empty except for a man standing next to the big door with his hands folded in front of him. He's wearing a lab coat just like yours. "Welcome to the Heidelberg Laboratory!" he says to the investors. "I'm Doctor Kessler."

The men walk forward and shake his hand formally. Kessler doesn't even seem to notice his daughter.

"In order to access the laboratory," Kessler tells the investors, "you must pass through our Decontamination Chamber. It is perfectly harmless, I assure you: just a little bit of steam and a computer scan, and you will be through to the other side."

He turns and punches a code into a keypad on the wall. You hear the sound of three massive bolts retracting, and the blast door slowly swings open. "There's room for all of you, come on now." He ushers the four men inside with a nervous laugh, then enters himself, closing the door behind him.

Penny crosses her arms over her chest. "Nice to see you too, father."

"I'm sure he's just nervous because of the investors," you say.

"Yeah, I'm sure that's it," Penny says. She doesn't sound like she believes you.

You go to the door to the Decontamination Chamber, where there's a computer screen on the wall. You can see the five men inside being blasted with jets of air. "It will only take a minute," you call over your shoulder. "Then we can go."

Penny is looking at the map on the wall. "Wow, this place is *big*."

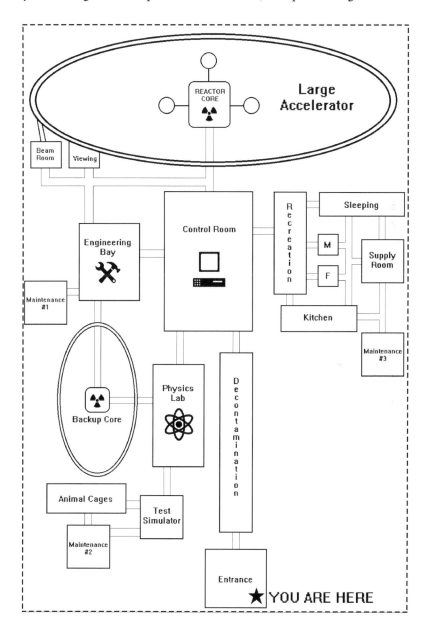

"It sure is," you say. You hear a computerized beep across the room. "Come on, it's our turn."

12

The door opens into a long, cylindrical room, with walls that curve upward toward the ceiling. It reminds you of a coke can on its side. There's a metallic echo as you step inside.

"Stand away from the door," you instruct. Penny obeys, and watches as the door closes behind you with a loud *KONG*.

"Hold your hands out to the side," you say while typing your credentials into the computer on the wall. "It won't hurt, I promise."

"Yessir, mister physicist, sir."

You frown. "Are you making fun of me?"

She bats her eyelashes. "Of course not."

You finish entering the protocol into the computer, and there's a loud whine like a jet engine spinning up. Nozzles in the floor and walls blast you with scalding air, fluttering your lab coat around like you're in a tornado. While that's occurring, a door opens in the ceiling and a device like a laser pointer sticks out. A single green laser beam shoots out of the end in your direction, then spreads out into a long fan-shaped beam. The beam moves up and down, scanning first your body, then Penny's.

The laser disappears back into the ceiling, and then the jets cease as quickly as they had begun.

You glance over at Penny and see that she's still gritting her teeth and squeezing her eyes shut. "All done, Miss Kessler," you say with exaggerated politeness. "There's no need to be afraid, now."

She opens one eye, looks around the room, then opens the other. She puts her arms down. "Do you enjoy scaring all the visitors, Jeremy?"

"Just the ones who tease me first."

She gives you a big grin. "I think I'm going to like you, Jeremy."

You turn away to conceal your own embarrassed smile, and press the button at the other end of the decontamination room. The far door opens with a hiss of air and pressure release.

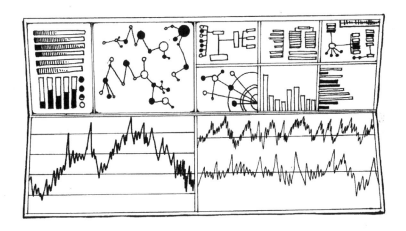

You gesture to the room. "Penny, welcome to the Heidelberg Laboratory."

Show her around *ON PAGE 25*

14

You lead Penny out of the Control Room and into the Physics Lab. You pause inside the door to look around. It doesn't look like there's anything in there, though.

"You sure there's not another CS Rifle in here for me?" Penny asks.

"Jay said this is the only one. Sorry!"

You make your way across the Physics lab and into the hall. There's a bend ahead, so you quietly stick your head around before continuing. The door ahead opens easily, no code required.

It looks like a movie room without the seats: there's a big projector screen on each wall, with the projectors hanging from the ceiling. There's also a stack of computer servers in another corner.

"This is the Test Simulator," you explain to Penny. "The computer runs simulations of what it thinks will happen, which are reviewed here."

"Okay..."

"You don't sound impressed," you say.

"Oh no. I'm *totally* impressed. All of this is super interesting, really." Her face is completely blank, until a corner of her mouth twitches in a smile.

Her sarcasm annoys you, so you walk to the other end of the room.

"Hey, I'm only teasing! Wait up!"

You open the door and stop in your tracks.

At the end of the hall stands a shining Phase Being, giving off the only light in the corridor. It's standing very still in front of the door, as if it's waiting for it to open.

You aim the rifle. It's a long way. Can you hit it?

FLIP TWO COINS!

If both land heads, *HEAD TO PAGE 37*
Otherwise, *FLIP TO PAGE 23*

"The shortest way is probably best," you say. "Let's head toward the Main Reactor hall."

Jay taps a keycode into the door. It takes him four tries, but he finally gets it. "Memory's still bad," he apologizes.

On the other side of the door are ten steps, leading down underneath the large loop accelerator. There's a lot of rock and rubble on the ground, like a stick of dynamite went off somewhere.

Straight ahead is the long hallway. At the end is a thick blast door leading into the Main Reactor. Jay stops and takes a long look in that direction. "See those cracks?"

You squint. "What cracks?"

"On the right, along the hinge. There's a black crack in the steel."

You see what he's describing: from so far away it looks like someone drew a line in sharpie across the shiny steel. "What does that mean?"

"Well, it's not *good*, young mister Heller. We'll worry about it after we get Penny. Come on."

Instead of going straight, you turn left down another corridor which leads to the Observation Lounge. This route was created so any important people or investors could see the blast door to the Reactor, as a way to impress them. But right now all you feel is uneasy.

And with good reason. As you turn left down that corridor you see a wall of rock ahead. Jay frowns. "Oh man. The Causality Neutrino really did a number on this place. A real number."

"Can we get through?"

Jay grabs some of the rocks and tries to move them. The rubble is too huge, a giant boulder blocking the entire route. "If we had a few hours, maybe. No point in doing that, though. Come on, let's go the other way."

He leads you back into the Control Room and then through the door towards the Engineering Bay.

Follow Jay *TO PAGE 31*

16

You think you know the right one. "Here goes nothing," you say.

Without waiting to consult Jay, you jump into the puddle with the white wire. There's a small splash, and then you stand there, frozen.

You turn back to Jay. "Whew! Glad I knew which one was safe."

Jay smiles and nods. "Me too." He follows you through the puddle to the other side.

You reach the end of the room, where the door leads to the hallway toward the Particle Beam staging area. Something out of the corner of your eye catches your attention. It's the strangest visual sensation you've ever seen. The air seems to warp, the way the desert heat drifts off the ground in waves, distorting everything behind. Then the strange object begins to materialize, thickening into mist, then into some strange sort of light. It's vaguely human-shaped, but made of what look like shards of light, angular and sharp, like chunks of jagged glass swirling in a small tornado.

"That," Jay says, "is a Phase Being."

"A *what?*"

"It's complicated," Jay says. "Now, we have a few options..."

If you have the CS Rifle, you can shoot it *ON PAGE 58*
Or, you can simply avoid it *ON PAGE 20*

You retrace your steps back to the Control Room. Jay looks up, surprised.

"No luck," you tell him. "Maintenance Room #1 had the radiation monitoring system. Not networking."

Jay shakes his head. "We need the networking system up!"

"I know, I know. We're going to try Maintenance Room #3 next."

Jay points to the wall. There's a square metal grate screwed into the wall at the corners. "We're running out of time. You guys need to take the air ventilation shaft. It will be quicker than walking."

Penny smirks. "The air vents? Seriously?"

Jay shrugs. "Why not? It worked in Die Hard. Come on, in you go."

You remove the screws and the grating. It's just big enough for you guys to crawl inside. "Just head in that general direction," Jay suggests, pointing. "You should reach the maintenance room at the end."

You lead the way, shimmying on all fours. The air shaft goes for about ten feet before splitting off. You pick the direction toward the third maintenance room.

Your wrists and knees make an awful lot of noise, banging hollowly on the metal as you move through the facility. There are grates spaced every ten feet or so, which provide enough light for you to see where you're going. You ignore the spiderwebs and piles of rat droppings that constantly brush against your arms.

The first ten grates you peer into don't look like the Maintenance Room. You pass the Recreation Room, one of the bathrooms, the Kitchen. Finally you come to a grate looking into a space that is identical to the first Maintenance Room. This has to be it!

Since it's screwed in from the other side, you kick the grate with your foot until it flies off, banging onto the floor below. It's not very far, about a fifteen foot drop. You and Penny peer into the room together.

"I can't see anything from up here," she says.

"Me neither. We need to drop down inside."

"How will we get back up here if it's the wrong room?"

It's a good question, but you don't have much of a choice. "We'll just have to be lucky."

You don't want Penny to think you're scared, so you swing your legs over and drop into the room.

Find out if it's the right room *ON PAGE 18*

18

You land on nimble feet inside the room. A moment later Penny drops next to you. She gives you a smug grin.

The room is identical to the previous one, with computer banks of dials and knobs covering three walls. You begin examining the instruments, looking for any clue as to what system this is for, but everything really does look the same.

"Let's just turn it on," Penny says. Before you can say anything, she throws the lever.

One light next to the switch flashes green for three seconds. Then more lights join it, and then the hum of computer fans and the clicking of hard drives, until the entire room is operational.

"Okay," Penny says, looking expectantly. "Figure out if this is the right one."

You squint at the measurements on the nearest screen. They don't really look familiar. Another screen doesn't give much data either. You move to the other side of the room and examine the data there. It's all just numbers!

Finally one dial sticks out. It says: **O2 Percentage**, and the needle is hovering around 30 percent. Next to it is another dial that says: **N2 Percentage**. That one is about 70 percent.

"O2 is oxygen, and N2 is nitrogen," you say. "The two most common elements in the air we breath. That means this is the Maintenance Room for the oxygen system!"

"Aww, man," Penny says. "Two in a row!"

"Only one place left to look," you say cheerfully. You stride over to the door. "Can't go wrong this time!"

The door handle won't move.

You try it again, but it doesn't budge. It's locked, and there's no way to open in from the inside.

Penny realizes what's wrong. She tilts her head back to look up at the vent. "Can we get back up there?"

You try lifting Penny up to the vent, but even on your tip-toes you can't reach it. She tries the door herself next, putting her foot up against the frame for leverage. It's no good. You're stuck.

Maybe Jay will eventually come looking for you. Hopefully that will be before the laboratory suffers a meltdown. But even if it is, for now you have reached...

THE END

You click on the word BEHEAD. A new line appears, then another, tapping out one letter at a time:

INCORRECT INPUT
CORRECT CHARACTER MATCH: 3
SYSTEM LOCKDOWN IN: ONE ATTEMPT

"Dang it," you say.

"But look, it has three characters in common!" Penny elbows you. "Come on, don't give up so easily."

"Okay, okay."

The screen now shows three options:

THREAD SHREWD RACKET

Which is it? This is your last attempt!

To guess **THREAD**, *HEAD TO PAGE 33*
To guess **SHREWD**, *TRY PAGE 107*
To guess **RACKET**, *OPEN PAGE 116*

20

"A Phase Being, young mister Heller, is a person who has been transplanted in time," Jay says. "The rogue Causality Neutrino we created is causing instability among the atoms in their bodies. So their atoms don't know *when* they are supposed to be."

"Hold on a second. Are you saying that thing is a *person?*"

Jay nods. "Someone working at the Heidelberg Physics Laboratory. Poor guy is stuck outside of time. Well, there's nothing we can do for him now. We can deal with him–and anyone else like him–later. For now let's focus on Penny."

You know Jay is right, but you can't help but feel sorry for the Phase Being. It has no eyes, but seems to stare at you pleadingly. Hopefully you can help it later.

As you slip past it, you notice something taped to the wall. It's torn, and all you can read is:

...THIRD PART OF THE SEQUENCE IS TO EXTEND FLOOD TUBES...

"Hey, look at this." You tear it off the wall and hold it up for Jay.

He reads the paper. "Huh. This is part of the emergency shutdown sequence. Hold onto it, we might need it later."

You now have **PART THREE** of the shutdown sequence! Be sure to write it down.

Leave the Engineering Bay *ON PAGE 80*

Thinking fast, you raise the CS Rifle and fire. It hits the middle of the three mice perfectly. It shifts and mutates and then disappears with a satisfying *PLOP*.

But the other two are still coming, and they've almost reached you. There's no time.

"What do we do?" Penny says. She's waiting for you to make a decision.

To try running to the Maintenance Room, head for the door *ON PAGE 43*

To jump onto an animal cage for safety, *HOP TO PAGE 96*

22

Just outside the door to the Control Room, the air begins to warp in an unfortunately familiar way. The three of you jump back just as the Phase Being finishes appearing.

Although it's difficult to tell since it has no face, it appears the Phase Being is staring at the door instead of you. It seems confused, and doesn't move.

Jay nudges you in the ribs. "You know what to do."

It would be embarrassing to miss from so close, so you raise the gun to your head and look down the barrel. You pause to exhale and then squeeze the trigger.

A beam of light flashes and strikes the Phase Being. It's frozen there as the light that makes up its body begins to flicker and tumble, turning into a recognizable shape. The image of a white-haired physicist in a lab coat smiles gratefully at you just before blinking out of existence, returning to his own time.

"Nicely done," Jay says.

You step forward. Something dropped from the Phase Being after it disappeared. You pick up a torn piece of paper that looks like it's from a textbook, or instruction manual:

> *...FIFTH, AND FINAL STEP IN THE SEQUENCE, IS TO PERFORM A FULL COOLANT DUMP. WHEN THIS IS DONE...*

You show Jay. "Oh yes, we'll be needing this," he says.

"For what?"

"Follow me to the Control Room and I'll explain everything."

You now have **PART FIVE** of the shutdown sequence! Be sure to write it down.

Follow Jay *TO PAGE 137*

It's a long way down the hall, and the light is playing tricks with your vision. The rifle shakes in your hands, the pressure of the moment getting to you.

With a final deep breath you squeeze the trigger.

PA-TEW.

The shot rings out with a flash of light. It strikes the door just over the Phase Being's shoulder, turning the metal black and leaving smoke dissipating in the air.

You lower the rifle. Shoot!"

"Come on, try again!" Penny whispers.

The Phase Being shifts. You get the impression it's turning around. You raise the rifle again and squeeze the trigger, but nothing happens, just a disapproving muted deep.

You look at the rifle. There's a small dial that says, "Recharge time." The needle is rotating down slowly. Oh no!

Penny asks, "What's wrong?"

"Come on, we need to go another way!" You grab her arm and turn right, rushing toward another door. Down the hall you go, quickly pressing the button to open the next door, throwing caution to the wind. You burst inside a dark room, and the door closes behind you.

There's a strange shifting sound in the room, but you know it's not a Phase Being because it's too dark. You feel around on the wall, looking for a light switch.

Penny finds it before you. The room suddenly brightens as the emergency lights on the walls come on.

"Ohh," you say, looking around. There are stacks of cages lining the walls. "This is the Animal Enclosure."

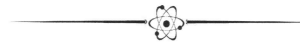

Check the room out *OVER ON PAGE 35*

24

You follow a narrow tunnel into the core of the Backup Reactor. It's a round room, with a circular hole in the floor in the center, about two yards across. You walk to the edge and peer inside. There's a metal floor on the bottom of the hole, with a series of long rods sticking out of it. A robotic arm holds one, slowly moving it deeper into the core.

"The main reactor will look something like this, but on a bigger scale," you explain.

"If we can find the missing sequence!" She shakes her head. "I still don't understand how a physicist like Jay could not remember what it is. That seems awfully strange."

You smirk. "A lot of what has happened down here is strange. I'm not surprised his memory is fuzzy."

Penny takes a step back from the core. "So where do you think we should–"

The speaker in the ceiling crackles with static. "*Hey you two, I think I miscalculated. We have less time than I thought.*"

"How much time do we have, then?"

"*Maybe ten minutes. We need to begin the core abort sequence soon. Have you found it?*"

You and Penny share a look. "We haven't. But if we keep looking I know we can..."

"*You've got ten minutes, max. Hurry up!*"

"I don't think it's in here." You point to the far door. "The Engineering Bay is through there. We could check there again, I guess?"

Try the Engineering Bay *ON PAGE 28*

The main Control Room of the laboratory is busier than usual. A dozen of the Senior Physicists scurry from one computer station to another, checking instrument readings and making notes on their clipboards. The entire far wall is glass, giving a view into a tube-like room beyond. The rest of the walls are filled with computer screens showing various graphs of data and video feeds.

"What's that?" Penny points to the glass wall.

"That's a section of the particle accelerator," you explain. "It's like a giant oval track, five kilometers long. See those ridges inside? With the coils? Those are powerful electromagnets, used to speed up the particles faster and faster."

"Ohh, cool," Penny says.

You lead her over to a corner of the room, where a single computer screen sits at a lonely computer desk. "This is where I work."

She blinks. "This is all you do?"

"Hey, I'm just an intern. I'm new. It may not look like much, but I still have an important job."

"Which is?"

"I'm in charge of monitoring the power levels for the facility," you say. "The particle accelerator has its own nuclear reactor. When we're performing our tests, the accelerator draws a lot of power. My job is to monitor this power level, make sure it's not drawing too much, and to notify anyone if the drain gets too high."

Penny raises an eyebrow. "That's it?"

"Hey, it's important," you say weakly.

"Heller!" someone yells across the room. It's your boss, Doctor Almer. He comes storming over. "Heller, what are you doing?"

"I'm just showing Penny around."

He swings his eyes toward her. "Who?"

"This is Doctor Kessler's daughter."

"Ohh." His entire demeanor changes. "Miss Kessler! Your father is wonderful to work with. Simply wonderful. You should be in the observation lounge with the other visitors." He glances at you, as if it's your fault.

Penny makes a face. "Can't I stay here with Jeremy? I don't want to be stuck with all those investors..."

Almer is dragging her away. What do you do?

If you want to let her go, *TURN TO PAGE 36*
Or, insist that she stays *ON PAGE 44*

26

"The living quarters is the only side we haven't been in. That's the plan."

Penny nods. "Let's do it."

You head east out of the Control Room, down a long corridor which opens up into the Recreation Room. There are couches in front of a television, a ping pong table, and a bookshelf in the corner. The wall to the left has a bulletin board and a jukebox. The room is pretty clean. No damage occurred here.

You point to the bookshelf. "See if there's any documentation in there."

While she does that, you head to the bulletin board. It's covered with personal fliers: one engineer is looking to rent out his spare bedroom in Zurich. A used 2003 Peugeot GTI is for sale. There's a safety notice about evacuation procedures, instructing employees to hide in the blast shelter underneath the Sleeping Quarters in the event of a meltdown. An order sheet for some scientist's daughter, selling Girl Scout cookies. You didn't even know the girls scouts were in Switzerland.

But there's no emergency abort sequence. "Any luck over there?"

Penny shakes her head without looking away from the bookcase. "Nope. It's all books for entertainment. Mark Twain, Michael Crichton. Lots of bestsellers..."

Suddenly there's a voice, coming from everywhere at once. "*Fifteen minutes, you guys.*"

It takes you a second to recognize it. "Jay?" you ask the air.

"*Neat, huh? I've got the PA system online. I can talk to you from here, and vice versa. But seriously, you have fifteen minutes to find the last sequence. So stop chatting with me!*"

Penny rolls her eyes. "I don't think there's anything here. Let's search another room."

There are four ways to go from here: the Sleeping Quarters, the Kitchen, and the male and female Bathrooms.

To search the Sleeping Quarters, *GO TO PAGE 147*
To search the Bathrooms, *TRY PAGE 149*
Or, investigate the Kitchen *ON PAGE 139*

You descend into darkness. Penny follows.

Jay climbs halfway down the ladder, then pulls the hatch closed behind him with a loud *clang*. You hear–but don't see–him twisting the wheel on this side to lock it into place.

For a long moment the only sound is your breathing.

There's a flick and a hiss, and a single flame appears in front of you. Jay is holding a flip lighter up. Its tiny flame barely illuminates the room: it's a small cube of metal, with enough room for maybe a dozen people. There's some bottled water and canned food stacked in the corner. There aren't any chairs.

"This room should withstand the blast of a meltdown," Jay says. His voice echoes in the tiny space. "Young mister Heller, why didn't you listen to me?"

The metal vibrates underneath your feet like an approaching freight train. The sound and shaking grows until you fall to your hands and knees. Penny falls next to you. The light disappears and you hear the lighter bounces across the floor.

The shaking goes on forever. Penny grabs your arm and squeezes it so tight you begin to lose feeling in your fingers. After several minutes, the shaking stops.

"That had to be the big one," you say. "Right, Jay?"

Silence answers you.

"Jay? Are you okay?"

Penny fumbles around on the floor for the lighter. It flicks on a few feet away, casting an orange glow around the shelter. Jay is nowhere to be seen.

For a moment neither of you understand. You look all around, but it's a small room and there's nowhere he could have gone. And the hatch door is still firmly in place.

"Where'd he go?" Penny asks, panic in her voice.

You never end up finding out what happened to him. Perhaps he was warped somewhere in time? But why didn't that happen to you and Penny?

The two of you hunker down and wait things out. You drink some water and split a can of cold tomato soup. You share a blanket and fall asleep hunched against the wall.

The hatch opens the next day, and search and rescue teams pull you out. You survived! That's all that truly matters, even though the facility is destroyed and Jay is gone. All things considered it's a success, even though this is...

THE END

28

You rush into the Engineering Bay, feeling more frantic than ever. You have to find the final piece of the sequence!

The room is a disaster, with half of the ceiling collapsed and debris and electronics everywhere. "Pick a pile and start looking," you say.

Penny takes the debris pile on the left, so you go right. You grab random pieces of electronics and toss them over your shoulder. There's just as much solid rock to sift through too, from the solid mountain on the other side of the ceiling. It's a reminder that you're deep underground, a long way from safety. If you can't find the last step to the sequence...

"I FOUND IT!" Penny cries.

She's holding a piece of paper in her hand. You read it:

> *...FIFTH, AND FINAL STEP IN THE SEQUENCE, IS TO PERFORM A FULL COOLANT DUMP. WHEN THIS IS DONE...*

"This is one of the steps we already have!" you blurt out. "We need step *two*, not five!"

Penny's face goes blank. "Oh. I got so excited..."

"If that's here, the other steps might be too." You begin digging at her pile, pulling out huge stapled stacks of paper. A lot of papers are too dirty or torn to read. Others have nothing to do with the sequence, and instead focus on the machinery in the Engineering Bay.

"Come on," you mutter as you use your hands as shovels, digging through the rubble. "Where is it?"

You both groan as the PA cracks on. "*Do you have it yet?*" Jay asks.

"No. But we're close, I know we can..."

"*Out of the question. Your time is up. Get back here now!*"

You want to ignore him, to keep searching, but you know he's right.

Time's up. *RUN BACK TO PAGE 82*

"Okay. Let's go rescue Penny."

Jay nods. "Couldn't have said it better myself. Now, which way do we go?"

There are two ways to the Observation Lounge. One way, the most direct way, is through the main door in the Control Room. That door leads to a tunnel underneath the particle accelerator, where it splits off toward the reactor core and the Observation Lounge.

The other way involves cutting through the Engineering Bay, then the Particle Beam staging area.

"The direct way would be easiest," Jay says, "but that takes us directly underneath the large loop. Since the Causality Neutrino went haywire there it might have messed up the tunnel, or created some other space-time tears."

"Space-time tears?" You don't like the sound of that.

Jay swings his head up and down. "Uh huh, young mister Heller. Space-time tears. You don't even want to know. Hopefully we don't encounter anything like that."

"If we go through the Engineering Bay we need keycode entry," you say. "I'm just an intern; they don't give me that kind of access."

"I think I can remember them." Jay grabs the side of his head. "My memory is slowly coming back."

"So which way is it?" you ask.

"Hey, you're the one who decided to help Penny first," Jay says. "And I'm still not feeling optimal. So you can call the shots, for now."

To go through the main tunnel, *TURN TO PAGE 15*

If you'd rather cut through the Engineering Bay, *GO TO PAGE 31*

30

You travel down the hallway and reach the back of the bathrooms. "I'll search the men's room, you search the women's."

Penny arches an eyebrow at you. "Scared to go into the women's restroom? Nobody's here, you know. You won't get in trouble."

"Hey, let's just focus on our task, okay?"

You approach the door. Unlike most of the doors in the facility, which are electronic and open sideways, the bathroom doors have a more conventional handle and lock. You give the handle a turn and yank...

It doesn't budge.

You pull again, and then bend down to peer at the lock. The deadbolt is in place, locked from the inside. Darn!

You walk into the women's room and Penny smirks. "Not afraid to come in here anymore?"

"Men's room is locked."

You search the room, but there's not much to see. Four stalls, all of which are empty. One of the toilets is missing, carved out in a sphere with part of the wall, most likely by the Causality Neutrino. Water dribbles from the exposed pipe and covers the floor.

"Let's backtrack," you say, realizing you're making no progress in there. "Maybe if we go check the–"

The PA in the hallway cuts on, faint but recognizable. "*TIME IS UP, I repeat, time is up. Have you guys found the missing sequence?*"

You and Penny walk into the hall. "No, we haven't," you tell the ceiling.

"Then there's nothing for you to do but get back here. Better run, you don't have much time to get to the surface!"

There's nothing to do but *RUN TO PAGE 84*

You travel down the short hallway until it ends at a metal door without any windows. Jay scratches his head, glances at you, and then punches in a code onto the keypad.

The door beeps, and then with the loud *ka-chunk* of disengaging locks it swings open.

The Engineering Bay is a mess. Fluorescent lights hang from the ceiling by their wires, flickering on and off. The workshop benches on the right side of the room have been turned over, and machinery is scattered across the floor. Part of the ceiling has collapsed in the center of the room, almost splitting it in two.

"Look at this," Jay says. He guides you to the left wall, where the metal covering is gone, revealing the rock of the mountain behind. You lean in and examine it; it's almost a perfectly circular hole. No, not a circle. A *sphere*. A half-sphere is missing. It's as if someone took a giant melonball tool and scooped out a section of the wall.

"What could cause that?"

"I'm afraid I know the answer," Jay says. "The Causality Neutrino is so unstable it's flickering in and out of existence throughout the laboratory. It has probably caused more damage elsewhere."

"Is there anything we can do about it?" you ask.

Jay gives a thoughtful look. "Maybe. We'll worry about that later. For now, let's focus on helping Penny."

You turn your gaze to the other side of the room. Since part of the ceiling collapsed, there are essentially two pathways to get to the far door. The right side has a thick power cable exposed on the floor, with naked wires sparking and crackling in the semi-darkness. But the left side isn't much better: although the pathway is mostly clear, the ceiling above is leaning precariously. It looks like it could collapse at any moment.

To go left, *TURN TO PAGE 42*
Or, take the right path *ON PAGE 56*

32

"Red's hot," you say, "which mean the black wire is safe."

Jay frowns. "Are you certain?"

"I'm pretty sure."

Jay opens his mouth to say more, but you're already turning away from him. Just to be safe, instead of jumping straight in you bend down and touch the water with the tip of your–

BZZZZZZZZZT

All the muscles in your arm go tense as they're blasted with electricity. There's a loud pop and you're thrown backwards away from the puddle.

For a long while you simply lay on your back, staring at the ceiling. You were so certain the black wire would have been safe! You don't know how you went wrong. I guess that's why you chose to study physics instead of electrical engineering.

Jay's face appears as he stands over you. His grey hair is standing on end strangely, and he holds up his hand to his face. The finger is black on the tip, with a tendril of smoke coming off. He must have gotten shocked too, somehow.

You'll probably end up being fine, but you're definitely too woozy from the shock to continue now. And that means this is...

THE END

"It's gotta be THREAD," you say.

Penny bobs her head. "I think so too."

You click on THREAD and wait. There's a long pause on the screen, and the click of the computer's hard drive.

INPUT ACCEPTED
NETWORK: ONLINE
SECURITY: ONLINE
REACTOR: ONLINE
ALL SYSTEMS: ONLINE

You throw your hands in the air. "Woohoo!'

Penny slaps you on the shoulder. "Nice going!"

Jay smiles and bends to the computer, typing furiously. Data flies across the screen in numbers and characters, too fast for you to see. "Well," he says slowly, "there's good news and bad news. Here's the good news." He points at the screen:

*...**FIRST STEP** IN THE SEQUENCE IS TO **DISABLE THE SAFETY** SYSTEM, WHICH WILL OTHERWISE ATTEMPT TO HALT THE...*

"Awesome!" you say. "But what's the bad news?"

"The bad news," Jay says ominously, "is that the reactor core is indeed close to meltdown. And we still don't have *all* of the sequence steps."

You now have **PART ONE** of the shutdown sequence! Be sure to write it down.

Listen to Jay's explanation by *FLIPPING TO PAGE 34*

34

Jay pulls up the reactor core monitoring program. It's a series of bars and percentages. Jay points to one of the bars. "The reactor internal pressure is at 92 percent. If it reaches 100 a meltdown occurs."

As you're watching, the number iterates up to 93. A few seconds later it hits 94.

"We've gotta get out of here!" Penny says. "It's about to blow!"

"There's one trick I can try." Jay begins typing furiously again, opening new programs and entering custom lines of code. You watch as a warning message pops up, which Jay closes. He punches in another command, and a *different* warning comes up. He closes that before you have a chance to read it.

He hits the enter key emphatically, then pulls up the reactor core monitoring program. The internal pressure is at 97 percent, and still rising.

Your immediate impulse is to bolt. You have to get away! Why isn't Jay panicking?

The bar stops rising, hovering around 97.5 percent. It stays there for a few seconds, then rapidly drops:

95

92

84

81

77

75

It hovers around 75 before stopping completely. "Jay, you did it!"

He shakes his head. "I only delayed it. I released the emergency steams valves. That should buy us some time."

"How much time?"

"I don't know. Half an hour, at least? It's tough to know for certain." As he says this, the number creeps up to 75.1.

"So now what?" Penny asks.

"Well," Jay says, "that depends on how many steps in the sequence we have so far..."

If you have four out of five steps, *HEAD TO PAGE 87*
If you have fewer than four steps, *TURN TO PAGE 132*

"Animal Enclosure?" Penny says warily.

"Yeah, we use them for some of the secondary testing that occurs in the Laboratory. Nothing bad, just harmless stuff. Measuring blood count after electromagnetic tests. Long-term effect of constant radio wave bombardment. That sort of thing."

"Uh huh." Penny looks into one of the cages. "Aww, it's just a cute little bunny!"

"We have rabbits, mice. Even a few cats. I named that guy Thumper." You smile, but Penny just gives you a blank look. "You know, the rabbit from Bambi?"

"Never seen it."

"You've never seen Bambi? Wow, we need to change that. I have to show you Bambi, it's a classic. Err, I mean, if you want to."

She gives you a coy look. "We'll see."

Something past her shoulder catches your attention. "Uh oh."

"Uh oh?"

You rush over to the cages on the far wall. Four of them are completely empty. "There should be mice in these cages. A few dozen of them."

"Jeremy... what's *that*?"

You follow her pointing hand and see something weird between two cages. The space is only two inches wide, but there's something glowing inside.

Before you can guess, a trio of tiny Phase Beings come scurrying out in your direction. They're hardly bigger than your fist, but they're fast little guys.

"The mice," you say. "Their Causality Neutrinos are out of whack too!"

The mice are training to be affectionate towards people. They're coming straight for you.

To try shooting with your CS Rifle, *AIM FOR PAGE 21*
To run for the Maintenance Room door, *DART TO PAGE 43*
Or, climb onto the nearest cage *ON PAGE 96*

36

With Penny gone, there's nothing to do but get to work. You examine the room. Already the air is filling with the excited chatter of technical speak as the physicists go through their pre-test checks, led by one of the senior techs:

"Proton source?" he asks?

"Proton source: active."

"Klystron generators?"

"Klystron generators warming up."

"Superconductive electromagnets?"

"Electromagnets A through J powered on, K through T standing by."

"Reactor coolant levels?" A pause. "Reactor coolant levels?"

It takes you several seconds to realize he's talking to you. "Oh, sorry sir!" You turn back to your computer terminal and examine the data. "Reactor coolant levels are stable."

The tech moves on without skipping a beat. "Diagnostics?"

"Diagnostics are nominal..."

You slump in your chair with a sigh. That was the extent of your job, until they run through the mid-accelerations tests. Just a verbal acknowledgment of the reactor coolant levels, and then monitoring the overall generator drain. Penny was right to think your job was boring.

Why couldn't anything exciting ever happen?

The door leading to the observation lounge opens, and Doctor Kessler strides into the Control Room. He's already balding in his forties, and his white lab coat hangs off his thin frame.

He raises his voice to address the room. "Okay, everybody," he says in his German accent. "I do not need to inform you how important today's test is. We have many prestigious investors in the lounge today. If we fail to impress them, we may as well close the doors on this laboratory for good."

He looks around the room, which has grown silent except for the sound of the computer fans.

"The goal of this test," he says ominously, "is to find proof of the existence of the Causality Neutrino, a sub-atomic particle never before discovered. If we are successful, today will be one of the greatest days in the history of physics."

He takes a deep breath and claps his hands together.

"Okay," he says. "Let us begin."

Begin the test *ON PAGE 52*

You aim the rifle in shaky hands. Ugh, why couldn't Jay be here to help you? You're just an intern!

You're wasting time, and Penny is counting on you. You take a deep breath, exhale slowly, and pull back on the trigger.

PA-TEW.

The shot rings out with a flash of light. You miss the Phase Being's center torso, but it hits one of the arm-like extremities, and apparently that's good enough. The Phase Being begins flickering in and out of existence, blue and red and purple, before becoming the image of a kindly old man wearing thick work gloves and a veterinarian jacket. Then he's gone completely.

"That was Bob," you whisper. "He's the animal handler."

"Animal handler?"

"Yeah, we have an Animal Enclosure just down the hall. Mice and rabbits and a few cats, for testing some of the effects of our electromagnetic research."

Penny makes a face. "I hate mice!"

"Well then we will just have to avoid that room," you say with a smile. You stride down the hall to where Bob just was and open the door to the Maintenance Room. "Okay, fingers crossed that this is the right one."

Check the room out *ON PAGE 100*

38

"I don't like the sound of space-time problems," you say. "Maybe we should get the CS Rifle. Just to be safe."

Jay points to a door. "That's the way to the Physics Lab. Follow me."

He punches the button next to the door and leads you into the corridor. Everything is awfully dark, with only the emergency lights glowing down where the ground meets the walls. Your feet echo on the metal floor. You come to another door, which slides open horizontally to reveal the Physics Lab.

It looks like something out of a college lecture hall: there are four rectangular tables with chemical-resistance black tops, with mounted lasers pointing at targets with computers connected at either end. A dry erase board stands at the front of the room covered in formulas and notes. The ceiling is exposed, with ductwork and pipes and wires. On the ground, there are stacks of printed paper *everywhere.*

"Ah-ha!" Jay grabs something from one table. "Here she is. The CS Rifle."

He holds the Causality Smoother Rifle up for you to examine. It's small enough to fit in a backpack, and the barrel is short and stunted. The grip is curved strangely, but seems to fit Jay's hand just right. Altogether, the CS Rifle looks like the lowercase letter 'd' on its side.

"How's it work?" you ask.

"Just like any gun: point and shoot." Without warning, he points it at the dry erase board and fires. The noise is tolerable, a low *pfft* sound, and a thick beam of light shoots across the room. It strikes the board and disappears.

"Nothing happened," you say.

"Uh huh. Nothing was *supposed* to happen, young Mister Heller," Jay says. "It only works on atoms in the wrong place in time. The dry erase board belongs here, so it stays here." He holds it out to you.

You feel its weight. "So I could shoot you and nothing would happen?"

Jay gives a nervous laugh. "Yes, *theoretically*, but let's not go testing that hypothesis today, okay?"

A static electricity feeling runs up your arms, making the hairs stand up. You're about to ask Jay what's wrong when a ball of pure energy pops into the room from nowhere. It crackles and hisses only a few feet from your head.

"Don't move!" Jay blurts out. "Stand perfectly still!"

ROLL A DIE!

If you rolled a 5 or 6, *GO TO PAGE 59*
If you rolled a 1, 2, 3, or 4, *GO TO PAGE 40*

Feeling confident, you type the command to power up the backup system, and then press enter.

The text disappears from the screen, and all that remains is a blinking cursor. You wonder if anything is happening.

Then the low hum of machinery reaches your ears, like a turbine turning on. There's a clicking sound in the air. You can't quite place it.

"*Looks like you turned on the backup power system,*" Jay excitedly says. "*Yes! That's needed because as soon as we finish the abort sequence, all power from the main reactor will cease. The backup power, from the secondary reactor, will keep things running now.*"

"We're doing it!" Penny cries.

There's a loud groan from the core, like giant sheets of metal being bent. You both freeze and watch the core warily until it ends.

"Better keep going," you say.

The options available on the screen are:

```
SELECT CORE FUNCTION
- FULL COOLANT DUMP
- EXTEND FLOOD TUBES
- OPEN CORE
```

"Do you remember the next step?" Penny asks. She's beginning to sound hopeful.

To perform a **Full Coolant Dump,** *GO TO PAGE 109*
To **Extend the Flood Tubes,** *GO TO PAGE 144*
To **Open the Core,** *GO TO PAGE 119*

40

You obey, standing as still as you possibly can. Jay does the same a few feet away.

The Causality Neutrino pulses in the air, its hum increasing in pitch every three seconds.

A crack of lightning suddenly shoots off, striking the dry erase board. It turns white, so bright that it's difficult to look at, and then fades away into nothing.

The Causality Neutrino blinks, and then disappears. But you can still hear the pulsing sound in the air. You glance at Jay but he has his eyes closed. You think he's praying.

The hair on your arms stands up again, your only warning. There's a crack of thunder behind you, and shadows swing across the room from new light. You know the Causality Neutrino is behind you, can hear the static sound, but you don't dare look.

ROLL ANOTHER DIE!

If you rolled a 1, *GO TO PAGE 59*
If you rolled a 2, 3, 4, 5, or 6, *GO TO PAGE 152*

"It's wonderful that you've found the full sequence," Jay says. "But I'm afraid I need to ask one more thing of you, young mister Heller."

You stand up a little straighter. "Anything. I'm here to help."

"Since the reactor core is unstable, it's impossible to open at the door. The safety systems are in place to keep anyone from entering. To manually override this, I have to stay here in the Control Room. You are going to have to be the one to go inside the core, run the sequence, and stop the meltdown!"

A shiver of fear runs through you. *You* have to be the one to go into the core? You're not prepared for that!

A glance at Penny strengthens your resolve. You have to do whatever you can. "I'll do it."

Jay nods as if there were no other option. "I knew you would. I can give you instructions from here. See that closet over there? Grab a suit from inside. It will provide basic protection from the radiation inside."

You go to the closet. Rows of yellow HAZMAT suits hang on the rack.

Penny appears next to you and grabs a suit.

"What do you think you're doing?"

She sticks out her chin. "What if something happens to you in there? You're going to need a backup. Two is safer than just one."

"But you might–"

"I'm going with you, and there's nothing you can do to stop me." Her tone and expression dares you to try.

You sigh. "Okay. Here, help me put this on."

You take turns helping each other put on the suits. It covers your entire body, with a plastic faceplate to reveal your face. It zips up the front. You feel like you're walking around in a suit made of trash bags.

"Go ahead down the tunnel," Jay says. "I'll open the door in a moment. And be careful! If you tear your suit, you're in trouble."

You open the door and walk down the long hallway. The massive blast door leading to the reactor looms above you. It's large enough for a tractor to drive through.

Clunk. Clunk. CLUNK.

The enormous locks begin disengaging. Slowly, swiveling with its enormous weight, the blast door opens.

Enter the Reactor Core *ON PAGE 102*

42

Electricity is not something you want to mess around with. You lead Jay over to the left side.

The ceiling groans as you approach, a hollow sound which reverberates throughout the Engineering Bay. You hesitate. The corridor between the wall and the wreckage goes on for about forty feet before reaching the door. It's a long way to go with the ceiling threatening to collapse above you.

You think of Penny, pinned beneath the wreckage, and it gives you a boost of courage.

Fearing to move too quickly, you tip-toe down the corridor. Jay stays right behind you, mimicking your stride. The ceiling shifts again, freezing you in place, but only a little bit of dust floats down.

You're halfway down the corridor when the air in front of you *shimmers*.

It's the strangest visual sensation you've ever experienced. The air seems to warp, the way the desert heat drifts off the ground in waves, distorting everything behind. Then the strange object begins to materialize, thickening into mist, then into some strange sort of light. It's vaguely human-shaped, but made of what look like shards of light, angular and sharp, like chunks of jagged glass swirling in a small tornado.

"Oh no..." Jay moans. "A Phase Being!"

"A *what?*"

"It's a–"

Suddenly the ground begins to shake. You whirl just in time to see the ceiling collapse behind you, piles of rock and debris falling into the corridor. It misses you by only a few feet, but when it stops you realize you're trapped!

The Phase Being extends what must be an arm in your direction. It lets out a low groan, sorrowful and sad.

"Don't touch it!" Jay says. "Whatever you do, don't touch it."

"What are we supposed to do?" you ask. It doesn't seem to be moving, just sort of standing there. There's about two feet of clear space to its right. You could try running past it.

Or, if you already have a CS Rifle, you could shoot it.

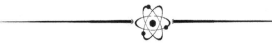

To try darting past the Phase Being, *FLIP TO PAGE 74*
If you want to look for something to distract it, *GO TO PAGE 51*
Or, if you have the CS Rifle, you can shoot it *ON PAGE 58*

Penny is practically shaking. "I hate mice!"

"The door to the Maintenance Room is right there. Come on!"

You grab Penny by the hand and lead her back across the room. The mouse Phase Beings make strange squeaking noises as they follow.

You reach the door and slap the open button. It flashes red. Nothing happens.

"Hurry up!" Penny cries. "They're *coming!*"

You press it again, and again, but it just won't open. You spin around. "We need to find another way. Or get on top of..."

Penny shrieks and bolts for the door you entered through, but there's not enough time. One of the Phase Beings cuts her off, colliding with her shoe.

She falls to the ground with a cry. The atoms of her foot brighten and float apart like dust. The brightness spreads up her leg, making her look just like the Phase Beings. "Help me!" she says, reaching a hand in your direction.

The wave of atomic instability moves up her arm and the hand drifts apart. The last thing you see is her wide eyes before she's gone entirely.

You hop onto the nearest animal cage, which provides safety from the little Phase Beings, but you feel defeated. You let Penny get hit. Now she's stuck somewhere in time! You feel a profound sadness, as if you lost someone very important to you, not just a girl you met mere hours before.

You might be able to continue and escape unharmed, but Doctor Kessler certainly won't be happy about you losing his daughter. Because of that, and since you're too sad to even move from where you stand, you have reached...

THE END

44

You reach out and grab Almer's arm. "Hey, hold on. Why doesn't she stay in here with me?"

Doctor Almer looks at you like you've lost your mind. "Are you joking?"

"I have an extra seat," you say, pointing, "and she won't hurt anything."

Penny nods vigorously.

Almer crosses his arms in front of his chest. "Heller. If you're making a joke, I'm not laughing. We've got the biggest test since this particle accelerator was built—we can't have visitors hanging around in the Control Room!"

"But she–"

"And even if we *did* allow visitors, we absolutely wouldn't allow the daughter of Doctor Kessler. Do you know what he would do if anything happened to her? Do you? I'll tell you. We'd be fired. And then Kessler'd probably throw us in the reactor room without a suit!"

He turns to Penny. "You don't want to get your boyfriend in trouble, do you?"

She grimaces. "I guess not."

"I'm not her boyfriend..." you begin to say, but Almer is already dragging Penny away. She gives a final wave and follows him across the Control Room to the door marked OBSERVATION LOUNGE and REACTOR.

Way to go, Cassanova. Time to focus on your job *ON PAGE 36*

You head into the Supply Closet. It's a small room with wire shelves from floor to ceiling, holding every manner of supply the facility could need: toilet paper and paper towels, spare linens for the Sleeping Quarters, pallets full of canned food and dehydrated milk and bottles of soda. Hanging from each shelf is a clipboard attached to a wire; inventory lists of all the supplies, with notes to indicate when replacements would need to be bought.

"I *am* hungry," Penny admits, "but I don't think what we need is in here."

You browse one of the clipboards just for curiosity's sake. As you do so, you realize there's ink on the back side of each page. They've printed the inventory spreadsheets on re-used paper. That's interesting.

You idly flip through a few pages, and freeze when you see one important part, highlighted in yellow:

*...NECESSARY TO **POWER UP THE BACKUP SYSTEM** AS THE **SECOND STEP** OF THE ABORT SEQUENCE, SO THAT POWER IS NOT LOST WHEN THE CORE REACTOR...*

You rip the page out and show Penny. "This is it!"

Her mouth hangs open. "I thought for sure we wouldn't find it! Yes!" She wraps you in a big hug.

When she lets go, you feel your cheeks redden. "Come on, let's hurry!"

You rush back through the living quarters until you reach the Control Room. Jay is bent over the computer. A red alarm is quietly pulsing in the background.

"Jay, we found it! We have the sequence!"

You now have **PART TWO** of the shutdown sequence! Be sure to write it down.

You did it! Now get to work *ON PAGE 41*

46

You type the command to power up the backup system and press enter.

The text disappears from the screen, and all that remains is a blinking cursor. You wonder if anything is happening.

Then the low hum of machinery reaches your ears, like a turbine turning on. It sounds like it's going well... until it abruptly cuts off.

The screen flashes with text:

```
BACKUP SYSTEM PREMATURELY INITIATED
        OVERLOAD POSSIBLE
     SAFETY SYSTEM OVERRIDE
```

Jay's voice chirps in your ear. "*What did you do? Did it work?*"

"I don't... I'm not sure. I powered up the backup system."

You hear Jay groan. "*No! That's not the first step! The first thing you have to do is disable the safety system, or it will just override the command and shut everything down!*"

"Oh, you just *now* remembered?" You can feel your heart pounding in your temple. "Okay, that's no problem. We'll just go back and start over."

"*You can't start over! It's going to put a thirty minute lock on the system!*"

You try the keys and realize the screen is frozen. "Oh no!"

"We've got to get out of here," Penny says.

"*You don't understand!*" Jay says. He sounds delirious. "*The system is locked. That includes the blast door! Ohh, why did you enter the wrong...*"

You and Penny realize what he means.

Despite what he says, you frantically run down the catwalk to the ladder, taking the rungs as fast as you dare. The reactor core begins to hiss, and the metal groans like a submarine. You rush to the blast door, but of course it's still closed."

"*I'm sorry,*" Jay says. "*I can't do anything for thirty minutes. I'm so sorry...*"

The reactor begins to rumble. Penny begins to weep. If only you had entered the sequence in the correct order. But you didn't, and that means when the reactor suffers a meltdown soon it will be...

THE END

You retrace your steps through the Particle Beam staging room–which Penny gawks at–and into the Engineering Bay. Before, there were only two paths for you to cross, but things look different now. Part of the ceiling has collapsed again, which has knocked aside some of the debris that was blocking your way before. Following the wall to your right, you now have a clear path around. You pass a door marked MAINTENANCE CLOSET #1 and continue around the side of the room.

You hear a noise around the corner, and hold up a hand to warn the others. Inching forward, you peer around a corner of wreckage.

There's a Phase Being next to a workbench covered with industrial power tools. It reaches out with a bright arm-shaped appendage and tries to grab a handheld drill. A strange thing happens where he makes contact with the drill. The surface glows yellow, like it's being melted. Then pieces begin evaporating into the air like ash flecks from a fire. The Phase Being's touch passes through the drill to the other side, essentially splitting the tool in half. The two pieces fall off the bench and onto the floor.

The Phase Being makes a strange noise at this.

Nodding to the others, you aim and fire the rifle. The beam hits it in the back–you think it's the back–and, like before, it slowly materializes into a solid shape. The shape of a young man with a black beard, wearing overalls instead of a lab coat. Then there's that same *pop*, and he's gone.

You rush forward to check for anything left behind. There isn't anything.

"Rats," you say.

"No piece of the sequence?" Jay asks.

You shake your head.

"What is that sequence for, anyways?" Penny asks.

Jay leads you through the doorway into the Control Room. "That's a good question. And I'm afraid, at this moment in time, it's the most important thing we need to do."

Find out what he means and *JUMP TO PAGE 22*

48

The men are uniformed, with rifles held across their chests and SWAT style helmets covering their heads. For a moment they're surprised by your appearance. Then they aimed their guns at you. They begin shouting in accented French.

You raise your hands. There's not much else for you to do. Behind them on the mountain top sit two helicopters, with men unloading gear from inside. In the distance you see three more approaching your location. Wow, this is a big deal! It's like a military invasion.

"Penny? Penny!" Someone pushes through the ring of SWAT members. It's Penny's dad, Doctor Kessler. He runs forward and embraces her. "Oh, Penny. I thought you were gone!"

She frowns and pushes him away. "How did you get up here? You left me down there!"

"Sweetie, I don't know what happened." He looks confused. "The Causality Neutrino went haywire, there were papers and debris flying in all directions... it felt like I was flying through the air, even though my feet stayed planted on the ground. Then suddenly... I appeared here. Up on the surface. We called the emergency response team, but everything was locked down. Even the elevator, until just a few minutes ago."

"The Causality Neutrino displaced you," you say. "You were stuck in time."

Kessler sees you for the first time. "Stuck in time? Who are you?"

"This is the man who *saved* me," Penny says. "His name is Jeremy Heller."

"He's just an intern," Kessler says dismissively. "He doesn't know what he's talking about."

"Sure I do. Jay told me..."

You trail off as another rumble shakes the mountain. Up high, with the other mountain peaks in the distance and the valley below, it gives you the feeling of being near a volcano when it erupts. The shaking goes on for several seconds, and knocks a few people to their knees.

Finally the shaking stops. "I think that was the big one," Penny says.

"Jay was down there!" you say.

"Who is Jay? What's his last name?" Kessler asks.

"Jay, one of the physicists. I don't know his last name. He stayed down there to try to stop the core from melting down. We were collecting parts of the shutdown sequence..."

Kessler scrunches his face up. "And did you succeed? The sequence is printed in manuals all over the facility!"

"I... we tried, but... there was so much damage and debris everywhere it was tough to find..."

Kessler rolls his eyes. "This is why I don't trust interns. You had a chance to save the facility and you failed." Suddenly he sees Penny's arm. "What on earth happened *here*?"

Penny look at her arm, which is red and blistered. "A Phase Being brushed my arm. It only took the skin off."

Kessler glares at you. "Not only did you fail to save the facility, but you failed to protect my daughter as well!"

"*Dad!* He protected me just fine. Without him..."

"Come on Penny, let's go." He takes her by the shoulder and leads her away, despite her protests. She sends one final look over her shoulder at you.

You want to run after Penny, but someone wraps a blanket around your shoulders and starts asking you questions. You answer them numbly as you watch Penny get on the gondola and disappear down the mountain.

You got out in one piece, so overall this was a success. But you regret leaving Jay, and wonder what will happen to the other Phase Beings stuck in time. Could you have saved them if you had found the final piece of the sequence? You also wonder if you'll ever see Penny again. Somehow, letting Penny go feels worse. It's a deep sadness in your chest, like you've lost something more important than you will ever know.

The Heidelberg Physics Laboratory is no more. But you're alive, and that's all that counts. One of the medics gives you a cup of warm broth, and it tastes salty and delicious. You put your face close to the rim to let the steam heat your face, and accept that this is...

THE END

50

"I have a feeling it'll be on the side of the facility with all the technical equipment," you decide. "Let's go search the Physics Lab again."

Penny gives you a nod of confidence.

You lead her south into the Physics Lab. It's just the way you left it: stacks of paper on the floor; a few lab desks with smooth black surfaces; the dry erase board at the front of the room covered in scribbles of notes. There's a cabinet along the other wall. Maybe inside–

Wait.

You turn back to the dry erase board. "Maybe it's written down on the board!" You rush there, excitement and certainly overwhelming your mind. You *know* it has to be here.

Penny appears by your side as you squint at the formulas and notes. A lot of it is math intermixed with letters as variables. Even though you got your degree in physics, a lot of this still goes over your head.

"I don't understand any of it," Penny says.

You keep searching, looking for any scrap of a sentence. In the upper-right corner someone wrote down what looks like a grocery list: bread, cheese, mayo. In the opposite corner someone seems to have written a reminder for the janitor to please *not* clean the board at the end of the day. Beyond that, there's nothing.

You sigh. "I thought for sure it would be in here."

Penny puts a reassuring hand on your shoulder. "It's okay. We'll keep looking."

Suddenly there's a voice, coming from everywhere at once. "*Fifteen minutes, you guys.*"

It takes you a second to recognize it. "Jay?" you ask the air.

"*Neat, huh? I've got the PA system online. I can talk to you from here, and vice versa. But seriously, you have fifteen minutes to find the last sequence. So stop chatting with me!*"

Penny rolls her eyes. "Let's search another room."

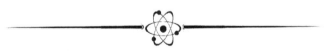

To search the Test Simulator room, *GO TO PAGE 141*
Or, head inside the Backup Reactor *ON PAGE 24*

"If only we had gotten the CS Rifle..." Jay says.

You look around, searching for some other option. The path behind you is almost completely blocked. For a brief moment you consider trying to climb up the debris, but there's no way that would work.

Not sure what else to do, you grab a piece of metal from the pile. It's about the size of a baseball. You turn back to the Phase Being, which is still standing square in your path. It hasn't moved at all.

You toss the metal underhand.

The metal arcs through the air toward the Phase Being. It's heading straight for its head, but before it gets there the Phase Being reaches out its arm-like appendage to catch it.

There's a flash of light the moment it touches the metal. For a split second tiny beams of light shoot in all directions like a disco ball. There's a strange ripping sound, like a plastic bottle being crumpled. Then the metal is completely gone.

The Phase Being lowers its arm.

You grab another piece of debris, and this time you toss it to the right of the Phase Being. The metal clatters across the floor. The Phase Being turns toward it.

"Now!"

While it's turned sideways, you dart around the other side. You slide past and are in the open area on the other side. Jay comes to a stop behind you. The Phase Being turns to face the two of you, looking strangely sad.

"Phase Beings," Jay says, "are humans that have been transplanted in time. The rogue Causality Neutrino we created is causing instability among the atoms in their bodies. So their atoms don't know *when* they are supposed to be."

"That's terrible! Is there anything we can do?"

"Well, my team predicted such a thing may occur, and we created a device to fix such errors in the space-time continuum."

"The CS Rifle," you realize.

Jay nods. "That's exactly right. We'll go get it after we rescue Penny."

Leave the Engineering Bay *ON PAGE 80*

52

"Beginning Causality Neutrino test," the head technician announces formally. "Initialize Injection Loop."

"Injection Loop initialized," someone declares.

Doctor Kessler grabs the clipboard from the head technician. "I'll take over from here," he says.

The head tech begins to protest, but Kessler ignores him and raises voice: "Fire test beam."

The largest screen in the room shows an overhead map of the particle accelerator. It's a big oval like a high school track, with a miniature track on the left side feeding into it. The proton is first fired from a beam in the smaller track, where it is accelerated around the loop to about half the speed of light. Then it is transfered to the larger loop, where it accelerates even faster.

The map shows the smaller loop flash green. "Test beam fired."

The head technician crosses his arms and looks annoyed at having his job usurped by Kessler, but he remains silent.

You look at your screen. There's a quick spike in the reactor drain before leveling off again. Perfectly normal.

Someone else says, "Confirmed test beam acceleration. All systems functioning nominally."

"Kill test beam," Kessler says.

The smaller loop flashes red and stops. "Test beam canceled."

Kessler nods his head. "Very good. Begin primary beam feed."

You open your mouth, and then close it again. Kessler was supposed to check with you for the reactor drain level, but he skipped the check. Thankfully, everything is normal.

The map shows the small loop flash green again, and then again. It flashes every time the particle completes the loop 10,000 times, which ends up being about once every three seconds.

Slowly, the flashing increases speed as the particle accelerates. It's flashing once every two seconds. Then every second. You know the next stage of the test is about to begin, so you return your eyes to your own screen to watch the power levels.

"Particle stability?" Kessler asks.

"It's perfectly stable, sir," someone says.

"Prepare to initiate large loop feed."

"Yes, sir. Initializing large loop superconductors."

There's a shuddering noise in the ground, like the Control Room was gently nudged by a giant's foot. The superconductors switching on. Those things are *huge*. The lights on the other side of the glass turn off, leaving just the glow of the coils of magnets. It looks like a stretched slinky as big as a commercial jet, glowing orange from all the power.

The sound repeats itself over and over, quieter and more distant, as they turn on around the large accelerator ring. The main computer screen confirms it: each section of the ring lights up until the entire loop is active.

"Large loop superconductors: active."

Something strange is happening on your screen. The reactor usage shows a series of spikes, up and down like a lightning bolt, indicating each superconductor turning on. That part's normal. But now that all of the superconductors are on, the power should be stable. It should be hovering right around 80% usage, barely fluctuating at all.

But that's not what's happening.

The power is continuing to spike up and down, like a seismometer during an earthquake.

Up to 75 percent.

Down to 45 percent.

Up to 77 percent.

Down to 48 percent.

Up to 82 percent.

Down to 55 percent.

It's spiking higher and higher, already brushing up against the upper safety limits. You look over your shoulder but Kessler has turned his back to you–he's now facing the computer screen and the windows. He was supposed to check the reactor status after the superconductor initialization, but he skipped that check.

The readings keep spiking. And the test is continuing without you.

"Feed loop is nearing transfer speed," someone announces.

"Superconductor tesla strength: ready."

"Proton analysis systems: ready."

In a few seconds, they're going to begin the proton transfer from the smaller loop to the larger loop. You need to do something, but what?

Maybe the sensor is wrong. Run some diagnostics *ON PAGE 60*
This is particle physics, and you're just an intern. Ask for help *ON PAGE 77*

54

You head back the way you came, one slow shuffle at a time. It takes ten minutes just to get halfway across the laboratory, and by then your back is killing you.

Instead of turning into the vent by the Control Room, you continue on toward the west side of the laboratory.

You pass a vent that shows the inside of the Engineering Bay. There's a four-way intersection ahead. You picture the map of the laboratory in your head, imagining where the Maintenance Room is. "It's this way," you say.

Penny says nothing as she follows you. It feels good to be trusted. Who's just an intern *now?*

You travel down a long ventilation shaft without seeing any room grates. Is there not a grate for the Maintenance Room? That would suck, having to turn around and go all the way back. Jay said this would be faster!

You see a diagonal shaft of light up ahead. There's a grate! "We're almost there," you call back to Penny, voice echoing in the tight quarters.

"Are you sure?"

"Pretty sure," you say, crawling forward. "And if I'm wrong then we can turn around and–"

The floor beneath your hands and feet gives way. You collapse straight down into a bright room, crashing onto the ground. A jolt of pain goes through your arms.

"Jeremy!"

You groan blink your eyes. You're laying on your back. Penny is still up in the air, looking down from the exposed shaft. Five feet of it collapsed under your weight. "I'm okay," you say, though your voice is shaky.

"What room is that?"

You look around and realize it's not really a room at all. It's more like a curving tunnel, with rounded walls and thousands of bundles of wire and cable around the outside.

You're in the large loop particle accelerator.

A noise echoes down the tunnel, like a power generator kicking on. The sound occurs again, and again, each time slightly louder. It's the electromagnets, you realize. Somehow they've turned on!

"Jeremy," Penny calls, "run!"

You get to your feet but collapse again from a sharp pain in your ankle. You can't put any weight on it! The electromagnets are turning on faster and faster, and you can see the sparks ahead of you. You're not sure what a super magnet would do to a person, but it can't be good. You look back up at Penny and wish this wasn't...

THE END

56

You don't like the way the ceiling looks on the left path. Better take the right.

As you approach the right path you see the floor is made up of thin square tiles, each separated from one another. Each tile is recessed into the ground about an inch. The path is four tiles wide.

Unfortunately, it looks like the sprinkler system went off here, too. Each tile has become a pool of water. Not only that, but there's the thick electrical cable hanging out of the wall and stretching across the floor. The cable splits off into four smaller wires which each disappear into a different puddle.

The outlet in the wall sparks with an abrupt flash of light. The electricity is live. "Be careful," Jay warns.

There are four wires: a **white** wire, a **black** wire, a **red** wire, and a wire made completely out of **copper**.

"We're going to have to step in one of the puddles," you say. "It's too far to jump."

"It's just like the wires in a house," Jay says. "Some carry a current, and others are safe."

"Yeah, but which is which?"

Jay gently touches his temple. "I... I'm not sure. My head is still woozy. You decide."

How's your knowledge of electronics? Do you know which puddles of water are safe?

Jump into the puddle with the WHITE wire *ON PAGE 16*
Jump into the puddle with the BLACK wire *ON PAGE 32*
Jump into the puddle with the RED wire *ON PAGE 95*
Jump into the puddle with the COPPER wire *ON PAGE 122*
If you aren't sure, turn around and go back to the left path *ON PAGE 42*

The Kitchen is a long, narrow room with stainless steel surfaces all along both walls, with space to walk down the middle. An industrial style ventilation system hangs above eight stove burners on the left. The ovens are on the right, four of them in a row, large enough to cook a meal for an entire facility full of scientists, engineers, and workers. Everything is clean and pristine, except for a single mixing bowl on the near shelf. You look inside: someone was mixing cookie dough. They must have gotten stuck in time right in the middle of it. It's a grim reminder of the disaster with the Causality Neutrino test.

Penny senses your mood. Wordlessly, the two of you begin opening cabinets and searching drawers. You find lots of utensils, pots and pans and cutting boards. One shelf has a row of cookbooks. They're mostly in German, French, and Italian.

At the end of the room, taped to a refrigerator, is a handwritten note:

Jessica, I swear, if you leave your leftovers in the fridge over the weekend again I'm going to put a padlock on the door! This kitchen is for everyone. It's not your personal food hiding spot.

After that, you've reached the end of the room. You've found nothing.

The PA in the ceiling cuts on. "*TIME IS UP, I repeat, time is up. Have you guys found the missing sequence?*"

You and Penny share a disappointed look. "No, we haven't," you tell the ceiling.

"Then there's nothing for you to do but head back here. Better run, you don't have much time to get to the surface!"

SPRINT UP TO PAGE 84

58

"Use the CS Rifle," Jay says. "Shoot it!"

"Are you sure? What's it going to do? What *is* a Phase Being, anyways?"

"A Phase Being, young Mr. Heller, is a person who has been transplanted in time," Jay says. "The rogue Causality Neutrino we created is causing instability among the atoms in their bodies. So their atoms don't know *when* they are."

"Hold on a second. Are you saying that thing is a *person?*"

Jay nods. "Someone working at the Heidelberg Physics Laboratory."

You look down at the rifle in your hands. "What is this going to do to it?"

"The Causality Smoother Rifle will reset the neutrinos in the Phase Being's body," Jay explains. "It will pop them back into the time where they belong."

"So it will make that person reappear right here?"

Jay scratches the back of his head. "Well. Err. Not necessarily. Just go ahead and use the rifle, then I'll explain."

You raise the rifle and aim it at the shimmering thing. It certainly *feels* like you're aiming a dangerous weapon at a person. You pull the trigger.

A solid white beam, thick and bright, fires from the barrel. It hits the Phase Being instantly. The shimmering shape begins to morph into more solid shapes and colors, like a kaleidoscope. Arms come into view, then legs, covered in a white lab coat. It's a man, you realize. His face materializes and for a brief moment in time you see all of him clearly.

Then there's a *pop*, and he's gone. A single piece of paper floats to the ground.

"Ahh," Jay says. "You see, the Causality Neutrino didn't just affect everyone here during the test. It affected some people who were working at the Heidelberg Physics Laboratory in the past or future. That man must have been from another time. Thankfully," he adds cheerfully, "you just returned him to where he belongs!"

You pick up the piece of paper that appeared. It's torn, and all you can read is:

...THIRD PART OF THE SEQUENCE IS TO EXTEND FLOOD TUBES...

Jay reads the paper. "Huh. He must have been carrying part of the emergency manual. This got left behind. Hold onto it, we might need it later."

You now have **PART THREE** of the shutdown sequence! Be sure to write it down.

Leave the Engineering Bay *ON PAGE 80*

You remain frozen in place, CS Rifle held across your belly. The Causality Neutrino pulses with energy, almost like a lighthouse, except you've never seen a lighthouse that makes such a strange humming sound.

A crackle of electricity shoots off the blue orb, striking a table. Its atoms turn bright white, spreading apart and disappearing into the air and ground like mist.

Jay doesn't look scared, but you can feel your body trembling. The rifle is heavy in your hands. You bend your knees to put it down.

Another bolt launches from the Causality Neutrino, striking you in the chest.

For a long moment you don't feel anything. There's no pain or discomfort.

Then the room begins to move, shifting side to side. Slowly it moves faster and faster. You feel like you're standing on a train platform while a train goes shooting by. Distantly you hear Jay yelling.

There's a high-pitched whine, then a *pop*, and then everything is different.

The room is completely empty of tables and equipment. It's just the floor and ceiling, the walls, and the three doors. The door leading back to the Control Room is open, and you hear the sound of pick-axes.

You walk in that direction and peer inside. The walls are exposed rock, and there's no floor. It's as if the Heisenberg Laboratory hasn't finished being built yet. Construction equipment attached to batteries are littered on the ground. The corridor only goes for twenty feet before ending at a rock wall, which two men are working on with pick-axes and drills. They're wearing hard hats and overalls.

One of them stops to wipe sweat from his face. He turns to the other and says, "La construction prend trop de temps!"

"Oui , trop longtemps."

They're speaking in French. You have no idea what they're saying.

One of them suddenly notices you. He practically jumps out of his shoes. "Qui es-tu? Que faites-vous ici?"

"Appelez la police!" cries the other.

You hold your hands up defensively, but they're already pulling out walkie talkies to call for help. You get the distinct feeling you don't belong there.

Hopefully Jay will be able to set things right back in the other timeline. But there's nothing for you to do until then, so you've reached...

THE END

60

This is a big test. You don't wait to freak everyone out over a false alarm. Maybe the sensors are malfunctioning.

You pull up the diagnostics program, which has some other methods of determining whether or not the reactor drain is legitimate. The first one is the main relay switch readings. All power to and from the reactor goes through the main relay switch, and it has its own method of measuring how much power is being pulled.

It verifies the same thing: the power spikes up to 85 percent, then down, then up to 89 percent.

You're still not certain, and want to exhaust every possibility before raising the alarm, so next you open up the reactor coolant levels. When power spikes in the reactor, the three coolant tanks automatically release their contents inside to keep the temperature stable. And they don't rely on the system temperature: they rely on a direct temperature reading inside the reactor.

And sure enough, the dial shows you, they're dumping massive amounts of coolant. Tank one is already almost empty! That proves beyond a reasonable doubt that something is wrong.

The power spikes are now brushing up against 100 percent, the top of the computer screen.

"Initiate large loop feed," Kessler says.

One of the techs repeats, "Large loop feed: initiated." On the screen the large loop blinks green once, confirming that the supercharged proton has entered the bigger track. Through the glass, there's a short flash of light and a low hum as the electromagnets pulse.

Next to your keyboard is a metal box built into the desk. You flip the box open to reveal a small red "abort" button. Pressing that would cause the electromagnets to immediately shut down and cause the supercharged proton to crash into the sides of the large loop. It would only be a minor burst, not enough to be dangerous, but it *would* damage some of the sensors and require weeks of recalibration.

But if you don't do it, and the reactor goes critical...

You glance over your shoulder. Your boss, Doctor Almer, is only a few feet away.

To avoid taking chances, immediately abort the test *ON PAGE 63*
If you'd rather call your boss over and let him decide, *FLIP TO PAGE 77*

You run to the door marked "BACKUP REACTOR" and follow Jay inside. A quick glance over your shoulder shows the Phase Being doesn't follow.

You're in another corridor, completely dark except for the red emergency lights in the floor.

"What's the Backup Reactor?" Penny asks.

"We have a smaller particle accelerator on site," Jay explains while leading you down the hall. "We use it to perform test experiments prior to using the large loop accelerator. The test accelerator has its own reactor dedicated to it and it alone."

"Isn't that dangerous?" Penny asks.

"Why would it be dangerous?"

"I don't know. I thought nuclear reactors weren't safe."

"Oh, they're perfectly safe," Jay says. "Just like a car is perfectly safe. Until you get into an accident on the freeway. This reactor, young Penny, is perfectly safe. Even now. But the bigger reactor..."

Your throat makes a *gulp* sound. "Actually, during the Causality test..."

Jay glances over his shoulder. "We'll talk about that in the Control Room."

You reach a metal door and Jay opens it with a pressurized hiss. You step into a tall room with a glass cylinder in the center, huge, like a thirty-foot-tall soda can. It glows faintly blue, and you realize it's the only illumination in the room besides the single computer terminal next to the door.

"This is the coolant tower," Jay explains. "If the reactor ever gets too hot, this is used to flood the reactor with chemicals to halt the chain reaction of enriched uranium. There's a second cooling tower on the other end."

"The primary reactor for the large loop has *three* coolant towers," you chime in, trying to impress Penny.

You continue around the coolant and to the door on the far end of the room. Then another corridor, exactly like the previous one. The lab is awfully monotonous.

The reactor room, however, isn't. It's another round room, with a circular hole in the floor in the center, about two yards across. Jay leads you up to the edge and you peer inside. There's a metal floor on the bottom of the hole, with a series of long rods sticking out of it. A robotic arm holds one, slowly moving it deeper into the core.

"Come on," Jay says. "The Physics Lab is just ahead."

Enter the Physics Lab *ON PAGE 150*

62

You sprint through the hall toward the Decontamination Chamber. The barrier looms above you, a massive blast door made of thick steel, designed to withstand a meltdown. The control panel on its surface glows with electricity. You punch in a few keys and, with a loud groan, it opens.

Once inside, you close it behind you. As you do, there's a rumble in the floor, vibrating up your legs. Penny looks at you. "What was that?"

"I don't know, but I hope Jay knows what he's doing."

Inside the Decontamination Chamber you're blasted with powerful jets of hot air from all sides. The normally inconvenient process is pure joy, now. The system confirms you're clean and the door to the lobby opens.

You rush to the elevator door to press the button. There's another rumble in the ground, stronger this time. The elevator car takes forever to descend, but finally it reaches your level, opening with a polite ding.

The ride up is just as long. Although the blast doors below are made to withstand a meltdown, the shockwave might still damage the area. You try not to think about what would happen to your elevator car in that situation.

But nothing happens, and the doors open on the surface. The frigid air of the Alps buffets you in the face as you jump out of the car.

And into an enormous crowd of people.

The men are uniformed, with rifles held across their chests and SWAT style helmets covering their heads. For a moment they're surprised by your appearance.

Then they all point their guns at you.

Uh oh. Hopefully you'll be okay *ON PAGE 90*

The numbers don't lie. The particle accelerator is drawing too much power from the reactor, and if you don't abort the test there might be a complete meltdown. Calling over your boss will only delay things.

Your thumb trembles as it hovers over the abort button. You take a deep breath, then a second one, and press down until you hear the button click.

You stare at your screen dumbly. There should have been a loud alarm, and the sound of the superconductors powering down, but nothing has changed. And the power is still at 100 percent on your computer, flashing red.

"Doctor Almer!" you call.

He comes striding over. "Yes, Jeremy?"

You point at your screen.

His jaw drops as he leans forward, squinting. "There must be some kind of mistake. Maybe the–"

"I checked the relay switch," you quickly say. "It confirms it."

"And the coolant tanks?"

You nod.

Almer wipes his cheek nervously. "Okay. Okay. We're fine here. We'll just abort." Before you can tell him, he reaches down and presses the small red button.

Again, nothing happens. "I already tried," you explain.

Almer looks back and forth between the computer and the abort button. Behind him on the main screen the large loop blinks green again, and again, each time repeating a flash from the supermagnet coils behind the glass.

"Doctor Kessler?" Almer says, licking his lips. "Doctor Kessler, I think you need to see this."

See what Kessler says *ON PAGE 64*

64

Doctor Kessler glances in your direction, rolls his eyes, then turns back to the main screen.

"Doctor Kessler..." Almer says, but his voice is trailing off. He's turning white, like he's about to faint.

You need to act fast. "Doctor Kessler!" you yell. "The reactor drain is too high! We're nearing a meltdown!"

That got his attention. He whips his head back in your direction, then comes running over. You point to the screen.

"We tried aborting, but it's not working."

"Of course it's not working," Kessler says. "I've disabled all abort switches for this test. The only way an abort can be initiated is from my desk, with my credentials."

"Doctor, we need to abort *now*," you say. The reactor has been stuck at 100 percent for a while now. There's no telling how long it can maintain that drain.

Across the room, one of the techs formally announces, "Particle is approaching the speed of light."

Inexplicably, Kessler doesn't appear worried. "This is obviously a malfunctioning terminal, or a malfunctioning intern." He turns his gaze to you. "There is no way I am aborting the test because of this."

"But *doctor...*"

He turns to walk away, and suddenly there's a loud groaning noise, like a ship's hull being stretched. You feel a vibration in your feet. Everyone looks around, confused.

Everyone except you. "Doctor Kessler," you say, tugging on his arm, "The instruments are telling the truth. We need to abort."

Without warning there's a flickering light across the room, like a multi-camera flash, except blue.

Kessler turns toward the flickering. "What was that?"

"It was inside the particle accelerator," someone says.

"It was a long streak of light, like a lightning bolt!"

"No, it was more like blue plasma..."

Kessler walks toward the glass, presses his hands against it. Terrified for your life, you get up and run to him. You grab his arm again, and open your mouth to yell...

The most peculiar glow appears on the left side of the glass, farther down the large loop, out of view. There's a flicker, and you swear you saw something zooming by inside the large loop.

Flicker.

There it goes again, rushing by from the left to the right. *Again*, it swings by, faster this time, a blur of blue across your eyes. And again. And again. Soon it's moving so quickly that it just appears as a single thread of blue string, suspended in the middle of the loop just on the other side of the glass. It's... beautiful, you think to yourself.

Everyone is standing up now, and several scientists are joining you and Kessler at the glass. You, along with them, are completely mesmerized.

The blue string seems to collapse, as if two people are pushing in on it from both sides, causing it to fatten and thicken and bunch up. Within seconds it's shaped like a glowing blue sphere, floating in front of you. The lights within the room flicker, but nobody notices, because they're completely enraptured by the object.

"Particle is at 99.999% of the speed of light," someone announces behind you.

The glowing sphere shimmers like weightless water. It pulsates, and there's still the quick flicker of light, and you get the impression that although the sphere appears to be floating still in front of you, it's actually moving incredibly fast around the five kilometer track. The way a car's wheels sometimes appear to be standing still even though they're spinning very fast.

"This," Kessler announces ceremoniously, "is the Causality Neutrino. We've done it."

The room breaks out in cheers.

Maybe the computer *was* wrong about the power. Find out *ON PAGE 66*

66

The physicists jump up and down, throw their hands in the air, high-five one another. You've never seen the stuffy group of scientists so ecstatic!

Almer clears his throat and glances at Kessler. "You see, *Jeremy?* I told you the power levels were fine. You shouldn't overreact to a malfunctioning instrument." Kessler doesn't seem to hear him.

You ignore him and point to the glass. "What's happening?"

The glowing blue sphere is no longer stationary, you realize. It seems to be spinning like a top, the edges of its surfaces shimmering strangely. Behind the sphere, in the large loop where the large coils of electromagnets form massive archways inside the tube, something is distinctly wrong. You squint inside and realize what it is: the bundles of multicolored wires, connecting power and computer sensors to all of the equipment, seem to be vibrating.

Almer sees it too. "It looks like the wires are shaking, like they're being pushed around by the wind."

Kessler snorts. "That's impossible. It's a complete vacuum inside the loop."

"I know, but that's what it looks–"

Crack.

A huge lightning bolt crack strikes the glass, cracking it from floor to ceiling. Smaller cracks begin to spiderweb off from it, extending to the left and right.

"What the..." Kessler says.

"The power," you say, remembering yourself. "We have to turn the power off!"

Kessler blinks. "But the Causality Neutrino. We have so much to measure..."

You ignore his argument and sit down at Kessler's terminal a few feet away. He's already logged in, so you pull up the main control program. A computer display of a switchboard appears, with dozens of multicolored buttons. On the left is a red one with the word "ABORT" printed in big letters.

You move the mouse to click on it, but Kessler grabs your arm, jerking the cursor away. "You little pest," he growls, "how *dare* you–"

The glass shatters.

The glass explodes inward, and the sound is as loud as a gunshot. The glass tumbles through the air, almost in slow motion, to be sucked into the blue orb. Your hair blows forward, as if the orb is pulling on every atom in the room at once.

The physicists begin shouting all at once.

The sphere is rotating chaotically fast now, with jagged spikes marring its previously smooth surface. It's like staring into the center of a tornado, or a lightning storm, or a blizzard where the wind blows so strong that it falls sideways.

You rip your gaze away from it. The room is mayhem, with papers and debris taking flight and shooting toward the sphere. Men and women in labcoats are shouting and screaming, arguing over what to do. Kessler's screen still shows the program display.

A new alarm begins sounding, high-pitch and fervent. It sounds like you are out of time.

Gripping the desk with one hand for support, you take the mouse with the other hand and move the cursor. You click on the big "ABORT" button, and a new window appears:

PRESS ENTER KEY TO CONFIRM TEST ABORT

You lift your hand off the mouse. It takes an incredible amount of effort, such is the strength of the wind pulling you toward the sphere. But before you can press the key, the entire keyboard floats into the air and shoots toward the orb. The cord snaps and whips across your right arm. The sting causes you to let go of the desk and tumble backwards, where you fall against another computer desk.

The rush of wind in your ears makes it difficult to hear. The orb is as bright as the sun now, painfully so, with jagged pieces of light extending away from it like tears in the fabric of space. You see Doctor Almer tumble into the air, do a somersault, and fall into the orb. He disappears.

In front of you, hanging onto a computer desk for dear life, is Doctor Kessler. His face is plastered with pure terror. He blinks as if he can't believe what's happening.

The orb brightens, expanding on all sides. You cry out, but the wind is too loud to hear your own voice.

With a final, sudden flash, everything goes white.

TURN TO PAGE 108

68

The Sleeping Quarters are like a military barracks. There's an aisle down the center of the room, with rows of bunk beds on either side. Personal lockers are mounted on the wall between the bunks. Long rugs cover the floor.

"Those lockers contain personal information," you tell Penny. "But, there might be technical info as well."

You split up to each cover one side of the room. The lockers have a small key-lock on them, but they're weak enough that you can just pull it open with a little force.

The first locker belongs to a woman: there's a box of makeup, a contact lens case, and a photo of a family of three smiling at a camera. It's a sad reminder that many of the people from the facility are still stuck in time.

But there's no sequence. You move on to the next locker: this one has a chocolate protein bar, a stack of postcards, and a box of cue-tips.

"JEREMY!" Penny suddenly shouts.

You whirl to see a Phase Being striding across the room. It doesn't see you–it's too focused on Penny, who is now trapped between two bunks as the Phase Being approaches.

Moving with instinct instead of thought, you unsling the CS Rifle and fire. The solid beam of white travels the distance instantaneously, striking the Phase Being square in the back.

It halts its advance on Penny. There's a flashing like camera bulbs as it morphs and twists, gaining color and shape. You see the outline of a young woman with short red hair, wearing a lab coat, and then she blinks out of existence. The sheets on the beds nearby blow back from the energy release, and then everything is still.

You rush to where she just was, but it doesn't look like she dropped anything. Penny meets you there and smiles sheepishly. "Thank you for saving me."

Before you can respond, the PA in the ceiling cuts on. "*TIME IS UP, I repeat, time is up. Have you two found the missing sequence?*"

You and Penny share a disappointed look. "No, we haven't," you tell the ceiling.

"Then there's nothing for you to do but get back here. Better run, you don't have much time to get to the surface!"

To listen to Jay, *TURN TO PAGE 84*
To keep searching, *STUBBORNLY STICK TO PAGE 69*

"No!" you say. "We're not done searching. We can find the sequence, I know it!"

The PA crackles. "*Young mister Heller, no! You have to get out!*"

But you're not listening to him. You've already gone to the next locker and are searching inside. A pair of reading glasses. A bottle of designer shampoo. A flip phone that looks like it's over a decade old. You toss all the items over your shoulder, then move on to the next locker.

Penny is still standing in the same place as before. "I don't know if we should be staying. Jay said..."

"We can't let the reactor core meltdown," you insist. "We have to keep trying!"

She gives you a skeptical look and then continues her search.

The next locker has a personal notepad. Your heart leaps and you rifle through the pages. There's notes on worker morale, with a list of employees and their total overtime worked. The next page has a diagram of two Hydrogen atoms fusing together to form Helium. You skim forward a bunch to a page of Christmas present ideas.

You throw it down angrily. "Not here!"

The door at the end of the room opens and Jay bursts inside. He looks furious. "What are you doing? I told you, we have to leave now! The core is close to–"

The ground and walls rumble like an earthquake. You grab one of the bunk beds to keep yourself steady. A few lockers burst open and spill their contents onto the floor. Eventually it stops.

Jay moans. "It's too late. The meltdown is beginning. We'll never escape in time now!"

Remembering what you saw on the bulletin board, you run to the middle of the room. A long rug runs along the aisle, and you pull it aside. There's an outline of a door on the steel floor, with a wheel recessed inside.

Jay smacks his forehead. "The blast shelter! I forgot all about it." He bends to the hatch and pulls the wheel until it sticks out half a foot. He tries to twist it, but it won't budge. You fall on your knees and help him, and together it groans and turns.

Jay pulls open the hatch. There's a ladder leading down into darkness. "Get inside, quickly!"

Take shelter *ON PAGE 27*

70

You head into the Supply Closet. It's a small room with wire shelves from floor to ceiling, holding every manner of supply the facility could need: toilet paper and paper towels, spare linens for the Sleeping Quarters, pallets full of canned food and dehydrated milk and bottles of soda. Hanging from each shelf is a clipboard attached to a wire; inventory lists of all the supplies, with notes to indicate when replacements would need to be bought.

"I *am* hungry," Penny admits, "but I don't think what we need is in here."

You browse one of the clipboards just for curiosity's sake. As you do so, you realize there's ink on the back side of each page. They've printed the inventory spreadsheets on re-used paper. That's interesting.

You idly flip through a few pages, and freeze when you see one important part, highlighted in yellow:

*...NECESSARY TO **POWER UP THE BACKUP SYSTEM** AS THE SECOND STEP OF THE ABORT SEQUENCE, SO THAT POWER IS NOT LOST WHEN THE CORE REACTOR...*

You rip the page out and show Penny. "We found it! This is it!"

"I thought for sure we wouldn't find it!" She wraps you in a big hug.

When she lets go, you feel your cheeks redden. "Come on, let's hurry!"

You rush back through the living quarters until you reach the Control Room. Jay is bent over the computer. An red alarm is quietly pulsing in the background.

"Jay, we found it! We have the sequence!"

He looks up. "That's fantastic!"

You pull the other piece of paper from your pocket. "We also found this. It says there's a *sixth* step in the sequence. Is that true?"

Jay squints at the paper. He looks uncomfortable. "I... err, I don't know anything about this, young mister Heller."

"But do you think–"

"I'm afraid that decision will have to be yours," he says. "I must focus on the main sequence. Are you ready to save the facility?"

You now have **PART TWO** of the shutdown sequence! Be sure to write it down.

It's time to be a hero. *TURN TO PAGE 41*

Thinking quickly, you grab Penny's arm and pull her towards you. The Phase Being lunges into the open space she had just occupied, and then falls to the floor. It leaves a trail of glowing material where it touches.

However, Penny still lets out a yelp. "It touched me!" She holds out her arm and there's a long, finger-wide groove where the skin is burned. There's a strange smell in the air.

You whirl to face Jay. "Did it... is she... going to be okay?"

"It looks like it barely grazed her. But we've gotta get out of here. Come on, let's go!" Jay says. He opens the door and leads you and Penny through while the Phase Being is still on the ground.

You run down the corridor, turning right to pass into the Particle Beam staging room. Not slowing, you turn down the next door toward the Engineering Bay.

Penny's arm was injured. You'll need to remember this for later!

Hopefully you'll be safe *OVER ON PAGE 83*

72

You head back the way you came, one slow shuffle at a time. It takes ten minutes just to get halfway across the laboratory, and by then your back is killing you.

Instead of turning into the vent by the Control Room, you turn left, heading toward the south side of the laboratory.

You pass a vent that shows the inside of the Physics Room. There's a four-way intersection ahead. You picture the map of the laboratory in your head, imagining where the Maintenance Room is. "It's this way," you say.

Penny says nothing as she follows you. It feels good to be trusted. Who's just an intern *now?*

The shaft veers to the right at an angle before continuing straight again. Any minute you should be above the Maintenance Room.

There: a grate up ahead, with a diagonal beam of light illuminating the air vent. You bang your way toward it, excited.

"Is that it?" Penny asks.

You squint into the room. It's dark, and you can't see much of anything. "I can't tell. We need to get down in there and hope the lights work."

The grate flies away under your heel. You swing your legs into open air, then slide off the edge, twisting and grabbing the vent with your fingertips. You're hanging in the air. It's difficult to tell in the dark but you think you're not far above the ground.

You let go. There's a agonizingly long drop through the air–which is probably only half a second–before your feet strike the ground. You bend your knees, softening the landing. There's a weird smell in the air. "Come on down, it's not that far! Don't be afraid."

Before you can finish the sentence, there's a rush of air in front of you as Penny lands. It feels like she's grinning in the darkness.

You feel your way until you reach a wall, and then what seems like a door. You touch the wall along the frame until you find the light switch. The main overhead lights don't come on, but thankfully the emergency lights set in the wall do, bathing the room in red.

Rows of cages line the wall, none of them larger than a television set. You realize what the smell before was: animal droppings. "We went too far. We're in the Animal Enclosure."

Look around by *TURNING TO PAGE 35*

You click on the word RACKET. A new line appears, then another, tapping out one letter at a time:

INCORRECT INPUT
CORRECT CHARACTER MATCH: 0
SYSTEM LOCKDOWN IN: ONE ATTEMPT

"Aww man," you say. "And look–zero characters in common. This is terrible!"

Penny has a considering look in her eye. "Not necessarily. The fact that zero characters are in common with the correct password might still help us!"

"Yeah, but look," you say. "All three of the remaining options have no characters in common with RACKET."

"Oh."

You close your eyes. "Man, how could I have screwed this up?"

"It's okay, let's just focus." Penny sighs. "Maybe we'll get lucky on this guess?"

The screen now shows three options:

BEHEAD   THREAD   SHREWD

Which is it? This is your last attempt!

To guess **BEHEAD**, *GO TO PAGE 78*
To guess **THREAD**, *HEAD TO PAGE 33*
To guess **SHREWD**, *TRY PAGE 107*

74

"It's not moving," you say. "Let's try to slip past it."

"So long as we don't touch it!" Jay says.

"I know, I know..."

You approach slowly, preparing to jump backward at the sudden sign of movement from the Phase Being. It continues its low noise, sad and electronic. As you get closer you feel the hairs on your arm stand up. The air is charged.

The Phase Being stands in place, watching.

Feeling confident, you quickly move to dart past it. But just as you do, the Phase Being reaches out his hand. You change your stride mid-jump and press back against the wall, but there's not enough room to avoid–

The Phase Being touches you with glistening, shimmering fingers.

Jay yells, "No!"

A shock goes through your body. Now *everything* is shimmering, not just the Phase Being. You feel dizzy, and can't feel your feet, as if you're no longer standing on them. The surrounding Engineering Bay distorts and becomes pure white, and the Phase Being is doing the opposite: it's becoming more clear, more focused. It's changing into something else.

There's a strange *pop*, the light blinks out all at once, and suddenly you're in darkness.

You cannot see anything, not even your hand in front of your face. The air is cool and damp, and you hear the distant sound of trickling water.

Without warning a light comes on, blinding you. You shield your eyes, and as things come into focus...

There's a man standing in front of you holding up his cell phone as a flashlight. He's wearing a white lab coat. A physicist from the lab, but it's not Jay.

"Who are you?" you ask the man.

"I'm Bruce. One of the electrical engineers," he says. "You... you're human? You were this strange shimmering light, all angular and shifting. It sounded like you were calling out for help, so I grabbed your hand..."

"That's what *you* looked like! Jay called you a Phase Being."

"Phase Being? Jay?"

He must not have seen the results of the test. "The Causality Neutrino," you explain. "The test worked. We were able to find it, but it was unstable."

Bruce looks at you like you're crazy. "What are you talking about? That test isn't for another six months!"

Six months? This guy isn't making any sense. He's probably disoriented, the way Jay was. Instead of answering him, you look around. From the soft glow of the cell phone screen you see the walls are made of rock, along with the ceiling and floor. You're in a cave. There's a narrow passageway extending away from you, but in the dark you can't see more than a few feet.

Bruce looks around. His eyes stop on the wall behind you. "Oh no."

You spin around. On the wall behind you are strange markings. No, wait. They're not markings. They're pictures, drawn in red and brown paint.

There's a picture of what looks like a large cat, surrounded by three men with long spears. The drawing is crude and child-like.

"Wow," you say, "these must be thousands of years old! Do you think anyone has ever discovered them before?"

Bruce leans close to the wall, holding out his phone. He touches the wall with a fingertip, rubbing at the picture of the cat. The paint comes off at his touch.

"I don't think anyone has discovered these before," Bruce says, "because these paintings are *brand new*."

It takes you a moment to figure out what he means. "The Causality Neutrino," you say. "Did it... move us? Are we in prehistoric times?"

Bruce doesn't answer. He sits on the ground and puts his head in his hands. "If we're... that means you came from... oh no. Oh no."

Maybe it's not so bad. Someone with your modern knowledge would do well in prehistoric times, right? And maybe Jay will find a way to rescue you, somehow. Who knows. But in either case, for now your adventure has reached...

THE END

76

"We've already been in the Engineering Bay," you decide, "so we know what to expect on the way to Maintenance Room One."

"Good idea," Penny agrees. "Plus it's the closest to the Control Room."

Still cradling his aching head, Jay says, "I'll hold down the fort from here. Hopefully I'm feeling better by the time you're done."

You share a look with Penny and then stride through the door.

The Engineering Bay is less exciting than before, with no Phase Beings to speak of. You cradle your CS Rifle and pretend not to be relieved.

"Are you sure Jay is alright?" Penny asks.

"I don't know. He seems shaken up, but he's not too bad."

Penny shakes her head. "No, not that. I mean... do you think he's telling us the truth?"

That takes you aback. "What do you mean? You think he's lying? What would he lie about?"

"I don't know, I just get a weird feeling. Like he's not telling us everything."

"Well, that's sort of true," you say with a grin, "since he's unable to tell us which Maintenance Room is the right one!"

Penny doesn't laugh. "There's something more. I can feel it."

"Hey, he was the one who correctly predicted this would happen. He tried to warn Doctor Kessler." You don't know why you're defending him, but it's a persistent need in your mind. You're certain he's right.

"Are you saying my father is to blame?"

"No, of course not!" you quickly say as you pass through the door and into another hallway. Although Kessler *was* the one who disabled the abort switch during the test. And someone had over-charged the proton in the Particle Beam. But you can't say that to Penny.

She groans as you reach the door at the end of the hall. "Looks like you chose wrong." There's a sign next to the door that says:

MAINTENANCE ROOM: RADIATION SYSTEM

"Darn," you say. "Oh well, at least it was a quick trip, right?"

To give Maintenance Room #2 a shot, *HEAD TO PAGE 94*
If your gut says Maintenance Room #3, then *TRY PAGE 17*
Or, if you want to check out the Radiation system anyways, *GO TO PAGE 85*

This is *not* a decision you should be making. You spin around in your computer chair. "Doctor Almer!"

He comes striding over. "Yes, Jeremy?"

You point at your screen.

His jaw drops as he leans forward, squinting. "There must be some kind of mistake. Did you check the main relay switch?"

"I wanted to notify you first."

Almer pushes you out of the way and opens the diagnostics program. He groans at what he sees for the main relay switch. Then he checks the coolant tank levels. You see over his shoulder that they're releasing coolant at maximum flow, which proves that the reactor is overloaded.

On the other monitor, the spikes reach 100 percent and the screen flashes red.

Almer wipes his cheek nervously. "Okay. Okay. We're fine here. We'll just abort." Next to your keyboard is a metal box built into the desk. He flips the box open to reveal a small red "abort" button.

The two of you share a look of fear before he presses it with his thumb, making a soft *click*.

You wait. And wait some more.

Nothing happens.

Almer looks back and forth between the computer and the abort button. Behind him on the main screen the large loop blinks green again, and again, each time repeating a flash from the supermagnet coils behind the glass. The test is progressing quickly, and the power indicator is now stuck at 100 percent. If you don't abort quickly...

"Doctor Kessler?" Almer says, licking his lips. "Doctor Kessler, I think you need to see this."

Get Kessler's attention *ON PAGE 64*

78

You click on the word BEHEAD. There's a long pause on the screen, and the click of the computer's hard drive.

```
        INCORRECT INPUT
  CORRECT CHARACTER MATCH: 3
    SYSTEM LOCKDOWN: ACTIVE
    SYSTEM LOCKDOWN: ACTIVE
    SYSTEM LOCKDOWN: ACTIVE
```

"NO!" you and Penny cry out at the same time.

Jay slumps his head. "That was unfortunate."

"What are we going to do, Jay?"

"Well. There's good news, and bad news. The bad news is that the system is completely locked out, so we have no way of knowing if the core reactor is going to meltdown any time soon."

"And the good?"

"The good news is that by you two bringing up the network, the Decontamination Chamber is active. The system lockdown in the Control Room doesn't affect that."

You and Penny look at one another. "So we can get out of here? Really?"

"Uh huh." He doesn't look very happy. "I had hoped to stop the reactor, and maybe even... ahh, well there's nothing to be done now. You two better hurry up and get to the surface."

"You're not coming with us?" you ask.

He waves it off. "I'm going to try one last thing and see if I can bypass the computer. I'll be right behind you guys, I promise. Go, hurry!"

You take Penny's hand. "Come on, let's go!"

Make your getaway *ON PAGE 79*

You sprint out of the Control Room and into the Decontamination Chamber. The door opens at the press of a button, and you both jump inside.

You're blasted with powerful jets of hot air from all sides. The normally inconvenient process is pure joy, now. The system confirms you're clean and the door to the lobby opens.

There's a low rumble in the floor which lasts several seconds. You and Penny share a *let's get out of here* look. She runs past you to press the elevator button.

"Come on. Come on!" you say. What's taking so long?

There's another rumble, deeper within the facility. "Jay had better get out," Penny says.

"He will. I don't know how, but I can feel it." You're practically hopping up and down waiting for the elevator, now. "Hurry up!"

With a ding, the doors open. You both jump inside, close the door, and press 'S' for Surface. The car jerks into motion.

You begin to relax. After so much excitement down there, it almost feels strange to be leaving. Like you're leaving part of yourself behind.

"Will we be safe on the surface?" Penny asks. "You know. If the reactor..."

"Yeah, I think so. They test detonate nukes underground, you know? A meltdown of our core would be a big explosion underground, but not much up here except for a rumble."

As if on cue, there's another rumble in the walls, much stronger than before. The elevator car bangs against the walls of the shaft, scraping with a wicked noise. You can hear the elevator cables swinging around inside the shaft, making a sound like a muted lightsaber.

And then, without warning, the cable snaps.

The lights go out as the car plummets, sending you and Penny into the air. Your head crashes against the ceiling, and then you're on the ground bumping against Penny. She's screaming. You're too confused to make much noise at all.

It's a long drop. You have a lot of time to think while Penny screams into the darkness. Strangely, all you can think about is that stupid computer system and the password you couldn't hack. You know if you had another shot you could get it right. But that will have to wait for another time, since the elevator car is about to crash into...

THE END

80

You're happy to leave the Engineering Bay behind you and continue down a short hallway. Only the emergency lights in the floor are working, illuminating the metal floor and walls in a reddish glow. Jay stops at the next door and punches in another code.

The Particle Beam staging room is the size of a small bedroom, and it's built for one single device. The particle beam laser takes up half the room, with a thick body in the center and a round barrel disappearing into the far wall. The frame of the laser is dull metal, but it's covered in exposed green circuit boards with wires crossing all over. The wall on the left is completely comprised of computer screens, knobs, and dials. Not only that, but the floor is glass, showing a view of the wires below. There's hundreds of them, thousands! Wires and power cables, all different colors criss-crossing and overlapping, like a pit full of snakes.

"This is where the magic happens," Jay says. "The supercharged proton is created and launched from here, into the small loop."

You already knew that–you *have* worked here for a while–but Jay seems to like to hear himself talk. "Okay," you say, "just one more hallway until we reach Penny."

But Jay is staring at the wall of computer screens. "That doesn't... One second, young Mr. Heller." He begins examining the computer up close.

"Come on, we need to get to Penny. We're almost there."

"No..." Jay says, trailing off.

"What do you mean, 'no'? We need to help–"

"I wasn't talking about that," he says. "I'm talking about *this*." He points to the screen as if that should explain it. When you give him a blank look, he continues, "The power. Someone cranked it *way* up. About twice the recommended amount. That would have supercharged the proton far more than recommended!"

"But who would do something like that?"

Jay pursed his lips. "I don't know. Someone who *really* wanted to find that Causality Neutrino." He takes a deep breath. "Okay, Penny time."

Head into the next hall *ON PAGE 92*

You lead the way, shimmying on all fours. The air shaft goes for about ten feet before splitting off. "The Maintenance Room should be just ahead," you say.

You continue for another twenty feet before reaching a dead end. There's one last grate right at the end, and nothing else. "Here's hoping this is the right room," you say.

You kick away the grate, which bangs onto the ground below. Lowering your legs first, you hold onto the side of the vent with your fingertips and drop, hanging in the open air like you're on the monkey bars.

There's nothing to do but let go. You fall through the dim air, bracing for impact. A jolt goes through your ankles and knees as you strike the ground.

Penny lands next to you a moment later. "Not afraid of heights?" you ask.

She grins. "Nope! Just mice. Now, are we in the right Maintenance Room or not?"

Examine the room *ON PAGE 100*

82

"Jay," you say as you burst into the Control Room. "You've got to let us keep looking."

He's busy banging away at the keyboard. "Get out of here. It's too late for searching."

"But Jay..."

"The reactor is going to meltdown! You have to go right this second." He grabs the CS Rifle from your hands. "Leave this here. I'm going to stay a few more minutes and see if I can delay it any further. You did your best, young mister Heller, but there's nothing more you can do. Please don't argue with me."

He seems strangely morose. The indicators on the computer show that he's right: the reactor core pressure is dangerously high. Reluctantly, you take Penny's hand. "We'll see you on the surface?"

Jay gives a sad smile. "I promise to see you in the future. Now get going!"

You sprint through the hall toward the Decontamination Chamber. The barrier looms above you, a massive blast door made of thick steel, designed to withstand a meltdown. The control panel on its surface glows with electricity. You punch in a few keys and, with a loud groan, it opens.

Inside, you're blasted with powerful jets of hot air from all sides. The normally inconvenient process is pure joy, now. The system confirms you're clean and the door to the lobby opens.

You rush to the elevator door to press the button. The elevator car takes forever to descend, but finally it reaches your level, opening with a polite ding.

The ride up is just as long. After several minutes the doors open on the surface. The frigid air of the Alps buffets you in the face as you jump out of the car.

And into an enormous crowd of armed people.

QUICK, THINK BACK! Did Penny injure her arm earlier?

If so, *TURN TO PAGE 48*
If Penny is unharmed, *GO TO PAGE 134*

You stop just inside the Engineering Bay. Jay turns and punches some numbers into the keycode. "There. That should lock the door."

"Will that stop it?" Penny asks. "Can't it just touch the door and, like, melt it? Like it did to my arm?"

Jay twists his mouth. "Well, yes... but the Phase Beings need to know they can do that. In reality they probably think everything looks normal, so it will see a door in front of it."

Penny touches her arm and lets out a hiss of pain. "So... am I going to be okay?"

Jay takes a closer look, but doesn't touch it. "It appears so. The Phase Being disrupted the atoms on the top layer of your skin, but nothing more. If he had grabbed more of you, your entire body might have become unstable."

"And then I would be like one of them?" she asked.

Jay shrugged. "Good question. Let's continue before we have to find out."

You examine the Engineering Bay. Before, there were only two paths for you to cross, but things look different now. Part of the ceiling has collapsed again, which has knocked aside some of the debris that was blocking your way before. Following the wall to your right, you now have a clear path around. You pass a door marked "MAINTENANCE CLOSET #1" and continue around the side of the room.

You're quickly tested again. There's a strange glow in the dim room and another Phase Being comes into view. He's standing in the doorway that leads to the Control Room. It looks like his back is to you.

"We need to go that way to get to the Control Room," you say.

Jay makes a face. "There's another way around, but we would have to go through the Backup Reactor for the test accelerator."

Penny looks at the pile of debris next to you. "We could throw something at it, distract it maybe."

Try to distract the Phase Being! Roll a die (or pick a number at random):

If you rolled a 1 or 6, *FLIP TO PAGE 104*
If you rolled a 2, 3, 4, or 5, *GO TO PAGE 110*

Alternatively, avoid it altogether by taking the alternate route *TO PAGE 61*

84

"Jay," you say as you burst into the Control Room. "You've got to let us keep looking."

He's busy banging away at the keyboard. "Get out of here. It's too late for searching."

"But Jay..."

"The reactor is going to meltdown! You have to go right this second." He grabs the CS Rifle from your hands. "Leave this here. I'm going to stay a few more minutes and see if I can delay it any further. You did your best, young mister Heller, but there's nothing more you can do. Please don't argue with me."

He seems strangely morose. The indicators on the computer show that he's right: the reactor core pressure is dangerously high. Reluctantly, you take Penny's hand. "We'll see you on the surface?"

Jay gives a sad smile. "I promise you'll see me in the future. Now get going!"

You sprint through the hall toward the Decontamination Chamber. The barrier looms above you, a massive blast door made of thick steel, designed to withstand a meltdown. The control panel on its surface glows with electricity. You punch in a few keys and, with a loud groan, it opens.

Inside, you're blasted with powerful jets of hot air from all sides. The normally inconvenient process is pure joy, now. The system confirms you're clean and the door to the lobby opens.

You rush to the elevator door to press the button. The elevator car takes forever to descend, but finally it reaches your level, opening with a polite ding.

The ride up is just as long. After several minutes the doors open on the surface. The frigid air of the Alps buffets you in the face as you jump out of the car.

And into an enormous crowd of armed people.

QUICK, THINK BACK! Did Penny injure her arm earlier?

If so, *TURN TO PAGE 48*
If Penny is unharmed, *GO TO PAGE 134*

"While we're here," you say, "why don't we check it out anyways? Maybe we can verify if the core is going to meltdown just from the radiation levels."

You enter the Maintenance Room. It's hardly more than a closet, with just enough room for both of you to stand inside together. The three walls are covered with dials and instruments, although currently none of the lights are on. In front of you, sticking out of the wall, are two side-by-side levers connected by a handle.

"Here goes," you say, pulling the handle down.

It makes a mechanical *CLUNK* as it falls into place. A green light next to the lever blinks for three seconds, then a second green light joins it, followed by a third. Then there's a soft hum as all the equipment begins powering on all around you.

"Too bad it's the wrong room," Penny mutters.

Not sure what else to do, you turn toward her and take her hand. "Look, I didn't mean to sound like I was blaming your father. I know you're scared for him, so I'm sorry if what I said came out wrong."

To your relief, she smiles. "Thanks, *young mister Heller.*"

You chuckle. "I don't know why Jay keeps calling me that."

"Do these dials tell us anything?"

You take a look at the nearest computer screen. "No, it looks like radiation levels are normal. That doesn't mean the reactor core is safe, it just means no radiation has gotten out *yet*. That will change if the core suffers a meltdown."

"Oh. Too bad." She points behind you. "What's that taped to the wall?" You turn and look. It's a torn-off sheet of paper:

*...MUST THEN **OPEN THE CORE** AS THE **FOURTH STEP** IN THE SEQUENCE IN ORDER TO...*

"Hey, we're in luck!" You show Penny the paper. "Part of the sequence. Alright, let's keep going."

You now have **PART FOUR** of the shutdown sequence! Be sure to write it down.

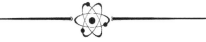

To try Maintenance Room #2 next, *TURN TO PAGE 94*
To try Maintenance Room #3 next, *FLIP TO PAGE 17*

86

"Let's try Maintenance Room #2," you suggest.

Jay points to the wall, where there's a square metal grate screwed into the wall at the corners. "You guys should take the air ventilation shaft. It will be quicker than walking."

Penny smirks. "The air vents? Seriously?"

Jay shrugs. "Why not? It worked in Die Hard. Come on, in you go."

You remove the screws and the grating. It's just big enough for you guys to crawl inside. "Just head in that general direction," Jay suggests, pointing. "You should reach the maintenance room at the end."

You lead the way, shimmying on all fours. The air shaft goes for about ten feet before splitting off. You pick the direction toward the second maintenance room. You ignore the spiderwebs and piles of rat droppings that constantly brush against your arms.

There's a grate ahead. "This is the Physics Lab. We're on the right track."

Penny picks up something off the ground. "Hey! Look what I found!" She holds it up, and you squint in the darkness:

...MUST THEN OPEN THE CORE AS THE FOURTH STEP IN THE SEQUENCE IN ORDER TO...

You continue for another hundred feet or so before reaching a dead end. There's one last grate right at the end, and nothing else. "Here's hoping this is the right room," you say.

You kick away the grate, which bangs onto the ground below. Lowering your legs first, you hold onto the side of the vent with your fingertips and drop, hanging in the open air like you're on the monkey bars.

There's nothing to do but let go. You fall through the dim air, bracing for impact. A jolt goes through your ankles and knees as you strike the ground.

Penny lands next to you a moment later. "Not afraid of heights?" you ask.

She grins. "Nope! Just mice. Now, are we in the right Maintenance Room or not?"

You now have **PART FOUR** of the shutdown sequence! Be sure to write it down.

Take a look around *ON PAGE 100*

"We've only found four steps," you say. "Steps one, three, four, and five."

Penny says, "We're still missing step two!"

Jay considers the computer. "We have about thirty minutes. It will take ten minutes to climb into the reactor and initiate the sequence. So that leaves twenty minutes to search the laboratory and find step two. But you'll have to be fast. I need to stay here and monitor the core, so it's up to you guys. Think you're up for it?"

You flash a thumbs-up. "Anything to help." Penny gives an emphatic nod.

"Where do you want to look? Jay asks. "Your guess is as good as mine where the missing step could be."

"Why don't we split up?" you ask.

"That's not a good idea," Jay says. "You only have one CS Rifle. Someone would be defenseless."

You realize he's right. There's no way you'll let Penny run around without protection.

"There's probably only enough time to search one half of the facility," Jay explains. "You could scour the west side, with the Engineering Bay and the Physics Lab and the Animal Enclosure. Or you could explore the east side."

"What's on the east side?" asks Penny.

"That's the living quarters for the scientists who work here around the clock," you tell her. "There's a recreation room, a kitchen, some bathrooms..."

"Either way sounds good to me."

Which way do you choose?

To search the west side of the facility again, *HEAD TO PAGE 50*
Or, explore the east side *ON PAGE 26*

88

"You're talking about time travel!" you blurt out.

Jay nods grimly. "Indeed I am. Chaotic time travel. You see, Causality Neutrinos are paired with atoms in nature. But what we did was unnaturally create one ourselves. It didn't have an atom to pair with, and all the other atoms in the vicinity had their own Causality Neutrinos to pair with, so..." He puts his hands together in a ball and brings them apart in an explosion gesture.

"Why didn't the physicists know it would happen?" you ask.

"*Some* of us did know. Or at least, we theorized. But we weren't listened to. Good. Now that you're up to speed, young Mr. Heller, we have work to do."

You nod. "Yeah. We need to get out of here."

"That's not what I mean. First, we need to look for survivors. I think we should check the Observation Lounge. There were several visitors in there during the test, like Kessler's daughter, Penny. They may have been unaffected."

You hesitate. "Are you sure? Shouldn't we leave that to the professionals?"

This seems to greatly bother Jay. "No! We need to do what we can. We have a duty to help. That girl–if that girl is in the Observation Lounge, we need to save her, and fast! That's Kessler's daughter. She's *important.*"

As if on cue, the intercom crackles to life. "Hello? Can anyone hear me?"

It's Penny!

You run to the wall intercom and press the button. "Penny! We're here in the Control Room. Are you okay?"

There's an agonizingly long wait before she responds. "I've been better. I could use some help, actually. I'm pinned beneath some wreckage."

Your heart leaps into your throat. "We'll be there soon! Just hang tight."

Jay looks at you approvingly, arms crossed over his chest. "That's more like it."

"So, let's go get her," you say. "I think we should..."

"Wait!" Jay throws up a hand. "It might be a good idea to grab CS Rifles from the Physics Lab first."

"What's a CS Rifle?"

"Causality Smoother Rifle. It, uh... sort of fixes problems in the space-time continuum. It's complicated. But trust me, we might need one."

Penny's hurt, and Jay says you might need protection. What do you do first?

To help Penny first, *JUMP TO PAGE 29*
Or, grab one of those CS Rifles *ON PAGE 38*

You type the command to extend the flood tubes, and then press enter.

The text disappears from the screen, and all that remains is a blinking cursor. You wonder if anything is happening.

Then the groan of machinery can be heard. You realize where it's coming from: doors have opened on three walls, below you, halfway to the floor. Slowly, a few inches at a time, the flood tubes are being extended from each of the three coolant towers. They crane across the open space beneath you until they connect to valves on the outer surface of the core.

The moment they touch, there's a flash of electricity. One by one, all of the lights in the room go dead, plunging you into darkness.

"*What did you do, young mister Heller?*"

"I extended the flood tubes from the three coolant towers."

"*Ohhh,*" Jay moans. "*Oh, that was very bad. Very bad indeed. You have to power up the backup system first, because as soon as the flood tubes extend all power drain on the main reactor ceases!*"

Oh no.

"Okay, we'll start over," you say. "Can I retract the tubes and start over?"

"*Of course you can,*" Jay says darkly, "*In twenty minutes.*"

"Twenty minutes?"

"*Yes! That's how long it takes to power up the backup system from scratch, and get all the other systems online. I can't even open the blast doors with the power out...*"

The blast doors.

Penny reaches out from the darkness to grab your arm. "Jeremy! What are we going to do?"

Jay is still squawking in your ear, but you've stopped listening to him. The darkness magnifies your fear. You turn toward the reactor core, which stills glows green, the only light in the room. Penny is talking to you too, but you're frozen, thinking about what it will look like when the meltdown occurs.

You failed to punch in the abort sequence, and it's too late to escape. This is very bluntly...

THE END

90

"Put the weapon down," someone shouts. It takes you a long while to realize they're talking to *you*. You're still holding the CS Rifle.

You drop the weapon like it's a rattlesnake. The men don't lower their guns, though. Why don't they trust you? Behind them on the mountain top sit two helicopters, with men unloading gear from inside. In the distance you see three more approaching your location. Wow, this is a big deal! It's like a military invasion.

"Penny? Penny!" Someone pushes through the ring of SWAT members. It's Penny's dad, Doctor Kessler. He runs forward and embraces her. "Oh, Penny. I thought you were gone!"

She frowns and pushes him away. "How did you get up here? You left me down there!"

"Sweetie, I don't know what happened." He looks confused. "The Causality Neutrino went haywire, there were papers and debris flying in all directions... it felt like I was flying through the air, even though my feet stayed planted on the ground. Then suddenly... I appeared here. Up on the surface. We called the emergency response team, but everything was locked down. Even the elevator, until just a few minutes ago."

"The Causality Neutrino displaced you," you say. "You were stuck in time."

Kessler sees you for the first time. "Stuck in time? Who are you?"

"This is the man who *saved* me," Penny says. "His name is Jeremy Heller."

"He's just an intern," Kessler says dismissively. "He doesn't know what he's talking about."

"Sure I do. Jay told me..."

You trail off as another rumble shakes the mountain. Up high, with the other mountain peaks in the distance and the valley below, it gives you the feeling of being near a volcano when it erupts. The shaking goes on for several seconds, and knocks a few people to their knees.

Finally it stops. "I think that was the big one," Penny says.

"Jay was down there!" you say.

"Who is Jay? What's his last name?" Kessler asks.

"Jay, one of the physicists. I don't know his last name. He stayed down there to try to stop the core from melting down. We were collecting parts of the shutdown sequence..."

Kessler scrunches his face up. "And did you succeed? The sequence is printed in manuals all over the facility!"

"I... we tried, but... there was so much damage and debris everywhere it was tough to find..."

Kessler rolls his eyes. "This is why I don't trust interns. You had a chance to save the facility and you failed. Come on Penny, let's go." He takes her by the shoulder and leads her away, despite her protests.

You want to run after Penny, but someone wraps a blanket around your shoulders and starts asking you questions. You answer them numbly as you watch Penny get on the gondola and disappear down the mountain.

You got out in one piece, so overall this was a success. But you regret leaving Jay, and wonder what will happen to the other Phase Beings stuck in time. Could you have saved them if you had hacked the system? You also wonder if you'll ever see Penny again. Somehow, letting Penny go feels worse. It's a deep sadness in your chest, like you've lost something more important than you will ever know.

The Heidelberg Physics Laboratory is no more. But you're alive, and that's all that counts. One of the medics gives you a cup of warm broth, and it tastes salty and delicious. You put your face close to the rim to let the steam heat your face, and accept that this is...

THE END

92

You follow Jay into the next hall. Ahead of you is the long corridor leading to the Reactor and the Control Room. The ceiling has collapsed, blocking the entire hall with debris. There's definitely no way through that from the other side.

Fortunately, the door to the Observation Lounge is just ahead on the left, with no wreckage in the way. Jay glances at you, stares off for a moment, then punches in the code.

Normally, the Observation Lounge is set up like the Control Room: the far wall is one long window giving a view of the large loop particle accelerator, and televisions are mounted in the corners so the physicists can show the guests different screens of data. A few couches and lounge chairs are spread throughout.

The room is a disaster. The glass is cracked in half a dozen places, but not broken. Most of the chairs have been overturned. One television has fallen off the wall to smash on the floor, while the other television still mounted has its screen shattered, the glass all over the ground below. Little pieces of debris and paper are everywhere, like after a tornado.

You see Penny to the left, far from the glass wall. She's pinned underneath one of the leather couches. "Hey there," she says with a weak smile.

You and Jay rush over and lift the couch. It's ridiculously heavy, and you can see why Penny was trapped! You manage to lift it enough for Penny to crawl out.

Jay stands back while you go to her. "Are you okay?" you ask.

"I think so. My legs feel alright, they were just pinned." She has a few cuts and scrapes on her face and arms, but nothing bad. "What happened?"

You and Jay share a look. "The experiment went poorly," you say.

Penny snorts. "Are you sure? I thought it was *supposed* to blow everything up."

It takes you a long moment to realize she's being sarcastic.

"It was strange," Penny says as she gets to her feet. "There was a glowing blue light, which excited the investors. They pressed their faces to the glass like kids at the zoo. But then the light began flickering, and then there was a blue sphere *inside* the room with us, and that's when everything started crashing around."

"The Causality Neutrino," Jay says.

Penny looks around the room. "So... I didn't really think about it before, since I was pinned beneath the couch and all, but... Where did everyone go? Where are the investors?"

Jay shares a look with you. "That, my dear, is a complicated question."

"Why? First they were here. Then they were suddenly gone. How is that possible?"

"The test was a success," you explain, "in the sense that we *did* create the Causality Neutrino. But it was unstable. We think it jumped all over the laboratory, disrupting everything near it."

"Yes, but where did the investors *go*?" Penny crosses her arms. "And what about my father? Have you seen him? You're avoiding the question. Is it because they..." She leaves it unsaid.

"You probably wouldn't believe us if we told you," Jay says.

"Try me."

You take a deep breath. Might as well come out and say it. "They're stuck in time. The Causality Neutrino disrupts an atom's time signature. So the people might be here, or a year from now, or way back in the dinosaur era."

Penny stares at you for a long while. Then she looks between you and Jay. "You're right. I don't believe you."

"Told you," Jay says.

"We'll explain it more later," you say. "For now, we need to find a way out of here."

Confusion suddenly spreads across Penny's face. She points over your shoulder. "What's *that*?"

Turn and see *ON PAGE 133*

94

You retrace your steps back to the Control Room. Jay looks up, surprised.

"No luck. Maintenance Room #1 had the radiation monitoring system. Not networking."

"We need to verify the *inside* of the core!" Jay shakes his head. "We need the networking system up!"

"I know, I know. We're going to try Maintenance Room #2 next."

Jay points to the wall. There's a square metal grate screwed into the wall at the corners. "You can crawl through the air ventilation system. I don't know if it's faster, but you'd probably avoid any Phase Beings along the way."

Penny smirks. "The air vents? Seriously?"

Jay shrugs. "Why not? It worked in Die Hard."

To take the vents, *CRAWL TO PAGE 111*
To use your feet, *WALK TO PAGE 14*

"Red seems like the obvious answer to be carrying an electrical current," you say, "but that seems *too* obvious."

Jay frowns. "What do you mean?"

"Well, things are rarely that obvious in real life. It feels like a trick."

"I don't know. I think you may be over-thinking it..."

You turn away from him. Just to be safe, instead of jumping straight in you bend down and touch the water with the tip of your–

BZZZZZZZZZT

All the muscles in your arm tense as they're blasted with electricity. There's a loud pop and you're thrown backwards away from the puddle.

For a long while you simply lay on your back, staring at the ceiling. Huh. I guess you thought it wouldn't be that simple, that red would actually be safe. That's why you chose to study physics instead of electrical engineering.

Jay's face appears as he stands over you. His grey hair is standing on end strangely, and he holds up his hand to his face. The finger is black on the tip, with a tendril of smoke coming off. He must have gotten shocked too, somehow.

You'll probably end up being fine, but you're definitely too woozy from the shock to continue now. And that means this is...

THE END

96

You grab her arm and pull her over to the nearest animal cage. It comes up to your waist. "Here, jump up!"

She scrambles onto the cage, and you quickly join her. As you turn around and look down you see that the mice are already where you were just standing.

Penny is practically shaking. "I hate mice!"

"Thankfully, it looks like they can't fly," you say.

"Yeah, but we're stuck up here. Now what? Wait for them to leave?"

You take a look around the room. Along the wall to the right is the door leading into the Maintenance Room. If you try making a break for it, the mice will almost certainly get you.

The cages extend that way for a bit. You could walk along the tops of them for a while, though you would need to climb because more are stacked on top. But then what? There's nothing over there but–

You smile. "There's another air vent up there. It looks like it goes in the direction of the Maintenance Room."

"I don't know," Penny says. "If we slip and fall we'd land on the ground next to those mice..."

"What other choice do we have?"

"We could stay here forever? And never move?" She gives a weak smile.

"You know we can't do that. Come on, Penny. I know you're brave. Just follow me."

Your words seem to invigorate her. You climb along the cages and she follows behind, slow but steady.

The screws in the corner of the grate come away easily. You look inside: there's a few spiderwebs, but that's it. "Here we go."

You crawl up into the vent.

See where the vent goes *ON PAGE 81*

Maintenance Room #2 looks the same as before: systems humming and beeping, lights flickering across the computers like a Christmas tree.

Penny looks around. "Where should we search?"

There's not much. No cabinets or drawers like the Test Simulator or Physics Lab. Just the computers and instruments.

Penny points to a clipboard hanging from a peg on the wall. "What about that?" She grabs it and begins flipping pages over.

You look over her shoulder. They're charts of names, dates, times, and signatures. "Looks like maintenance logs of who worked in here."

Penny puts the clipboard back. "Okay, so this was a dead end. Maybe if we run we can look in the other–"

The PA squawks. "*No more time, you two. Get back to the Control Room on the double. You've got to evacuate.*"

"But Jay..."

"*NOW.*"

Time's up. Hurry back *TO PAGE 82*

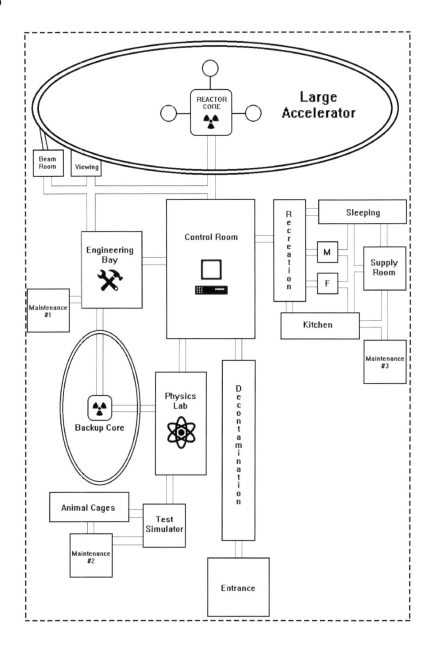

Jay points to the map. "There are three Maintenance Rooms here at the laboratory: one off of the Engineering Bay, one down by the Animal Enclosures, and one attached to the laboratory living quarters. They control the computer network, the laboratory oxygen levels, and the laboratory radiation levels."

You groan. "We have to go to all three?"

"No, of course not! That would be impossible in the amount of time we have. We only need to go to the one that houses the networking equipment."

"Whew." You and Penny look at each other with relief. "So which one is that?"

Jay shrugs. "Heck if I know."

"Wait, what? You don't know?"

"I'm still woozy from the explosion!" he protests. "I think it might be the one by... wait, no, I was *certain* it was the one with the... oh dear. Yes, I cannot be certain." He holds the side of his head and winces.

Penny frowns with concern. "You're awfully pale in the face. Maybe you should sit down." She reaches out to steady him.

He recoils from her hand and then looks at both of you with surprise. He blinks his eyes rapidly before abruptly sitting in the chair behind him. "Yes, sitting helps. In fact, maybe I should stay here in the Control Room while the two of you power up the network."

"Yeah, okay," you say. "Just tell us what to do."

"It's easy. There's a lever you throw to power on the system. It'll power on and do everything else automatically, which I'll be able to verify from here. And the system will say 'Network' on it, so you'll know if you get to the right one."

"Simple enough," you say.

"If we can find the right Maintenance Room." She turns to the map. "What do you think?"

To choose Maintenance Room #1, *SHOOT BACK TO PAGE 76*
To choose Maintenance Room #2, *HEAD OVER TO PAGE 86*
To choose Maintenance Room #3, *GET GOING TO PAGE 117*

100

You feel your way around the wall until finding the light switch. You flick it up.

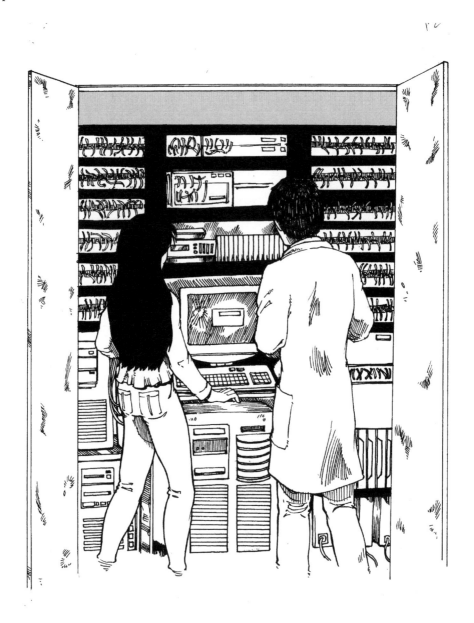

"Hey, we're in business!" Penny says. "Now what?"

You go to the first bank of computers. There's a two-lever switch that looks like the throttle for an airplane. "Do you want to do the honors?" you ask.

"Nope, I do not. That's all you, physics boy."

Blushing at her comment, you turn and push the levers up until they slide into place with a loud *KA-CHUNK.*

Lights come on around the room, green and red and flickering at different speeds. The whir of computer fans drifts deep from inside the servers. There's a faint clicking from what sound like hard drives.

One indicator on the wall sticks out to you:

```
NETWORK SYSTEMS ONLINE:
1. Main Reactor
2. Control Room
3. Engineering Bay
4. Physics Wing
5. Living Quarters
```

Each system has a light next to it. Only the Main Reactor light is on, a steady green color that you assume is a good sign. Then the Control Room light blinks a few times before becoming solid, then the Engineering Bay. The last two turn on simultaneously.

"I think that's it," you say. "Let's go see if Jay has everything working in the Control Room."

Head back to *PAGE 118*

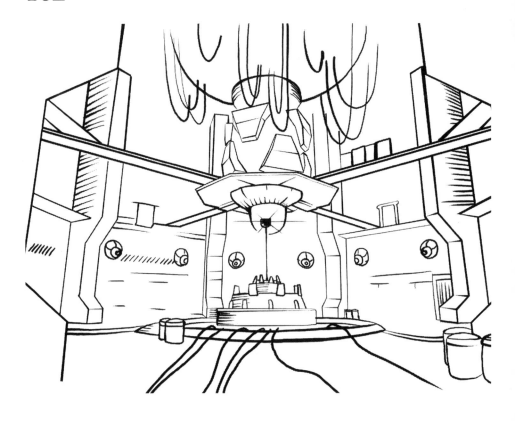

The core towers before you, atop a metal cylinder a hundred feet tall. It's made of thick metal, but tinted windows are scattered across its surface, giving a view of the green glow within. The ground at the base is covered with thick cables, like the black roots of some enormous redwood tree. The outer walls are filled with computers. High above, catwalks extend away from the top of the core in the shape of an X.

Behind you, the blast doors close again. Just a precaution, you tell yourself. It's just in case things don't go well. But things *were* going to go well. Right?

There's a single ladder mounted along the wall, rising precipitously into the air until it reaches one of the catwalks. You crane your head to look up at it. You can taste bile at the back of your mouth.

Penny is staring up at it, too. "We don't have to go up there, do we?"

A voice inside your suit cuts on, clear as water. "*I'm afraid so, my dear Penny.*"

You both look surprised, until you realize there's a speaker inside your suit. "Can you hear us?" you ask.

"*Sure can. Now, that ladder. It's the only way to get to the reactor core administration terminal. It's up at the top of the core.*"

You look up and see a computer-like object, in the section above the core where the four catwalks meet.

You take a deep breath. "It's a good thing I'm not afraid of heights."

"*Now's not the time for jokes, young mister Heller!*"

You shamble over to the ladder and grip one of the rungs. The plastic material of the suit you're wearing gives you a slippery grip. You put one foot on the lowest rung, testing the weight.

There's no use delaying. You take one step up, then another.

Climb the ladder *UP TO PAGE 145*

104

Penny's idea sounds best. You bob your head. "Yeah, let's distract it. Good thinking."

Penny beams.

"It's important that we choose the right item," Jay begins to lecture, but you've already found what you want. There's a cube-shaped circuit on the pile of debris, about the size of a baseball. Perfect throwing size.

"Watch this," you tell Penny.

You pick up the circuit and pull back your arm. You hear Jay yell, "Wait!" right as you catapult your arm forward.

The cube soars through the air. You aimed to the right of the Phase Being, but it must have heard you because it whirls around with impossible reflexes. Its club of a hand snatches the cube out of the air.

And the cube explodes.

It's an explosion not of fire, but of light and sound, blinding you and knocking you to your knees. For a long moment all you see is white.

When your eyes open, the Phase Being is grabbing you.

Everything is moving except you and *it.* It doesn't make sense, but it's how you perceive it: the floor and walls, the laboratory, even the *mountain* rush away and come back in a blink, changing, rusting, collecting dust. Time passes. Slowly the Phase Being materializes into focus.

When it finally stops you're still in the lab, but everything is different.

There's a musty odor to the air, like an Atraharsi tomb unopened for centuries. The lights are dim, the bulbs in the ceiling covered with a thick layer of dust. You cough, and suddenly the air blossoms with drifting particles.

Penny is there, along with a young man with a black beard, wearing overalls instead of a lab coat. His wide eyes spin around, taking in the surroundings.

"Who... are you?" he asks. "Where did you come from?"

"I was going to ask you the same thing!"

He checks the door. It won't open. "Only the emergency light is on," he says. "The doors are all out. We're stuck here!"

"What you mean, *stuck* here?"

But he's not listening to you anymore, and is checking the computer terminals. They're all dead.

A flip calendar on the nearest desk sticks out. You brush off a layer of dust and flip the page. The date shows in printed black lettering: **APRIL 14, 2085.**

Penny looks to you with fear, and you realize you've made a huge mistake. Jay was right about being stuck in time. Maybe you'll find a way back to the correct year, but for now this is...

THE END

106

"Animal Enclosure," you say, feeling panicked. "It's our last shot."

Penny hesitates. "But I told you I don't like mice..."

There's no time to waste arguing. You head down the hallway in that direction, and Penny quickly catches up. You stride into the room with a sense of urgency.

Three white objects fly across the floor, faster than any animal ought to move. Phase Beings, but of the laboratory test mice!

You take a step back but bump into Penny. She shrieks in your ear as she sees what's coming. You spin around just in time to see the door close. Your fingers fumble on the keypad, frantically pressing keys.

Penny screams louder. "They're at our feet! *MAKE THEM GO AWAY!*"

You feel a tingling sensation in your feet, and as you look down you realize you're falling apart. The atoms of your right leg have turned white and are spreading outward like steam in the shower. Penny grabs your arm tightly, and you realize the same thing is happening to her. You both share one final terrified look as the room spins and swirls, rushing away from you in all directions, moving through space and time.

Everything stops.

You're standing in the Animal Enclosure, but everything is different. The lights are all on, giving the room a clean, hospital feel. The cages are arranged differently: new clusters have been erected by the door. Most of them hold rabbits.

Penny screams and points.

On the ground in front of you is a white mouse. It's no longer a Phase Being. Penny's scream must have frightened it, because it bolts in a random direction.

Two scientists appear behind you. They're older, and their lab coats have a strange badge on the breast. Not only that, but the security door leading into the room is far more technologically advanced then before. Instead of a solid door, it's an opaque green membrane. The scientists step through and hold their hands out.

"Who are you? What are you doing here?"

"Sarah, look at their clothes. Nobody has worn that in decades..."

Sarah touches the side of her ear. "Security!"

Penny is still trembling in your arms. She's looking to you for help. You have no idea how you're going to get out of this one, and it probably is...

THE END

You click on the word SHREWD. There's a long pause on the screen, and the click of the computer's hard drive.

```
          INCORRECT INPUT
   CORRECT CHARACTER MATCH:  4
     SYSTEM LOCKDOWN: ACTIVE
     SYSTEM LOCKDOWN: ACTIVE
     SYSTEM LOCKDOWN: ACTIVE
```

"NO!" you cry out. "Four correct? We were so close!"

Jay slumps his head. "Well. There's good news, and bad news. The bad news is that the system is completely locked out, so we have no way of knowing if the core reactor is going to meltdown any time soon."

"And the good?"

"The good news is that by you two bringing up the network, the Decontamination Chamber is active. The system lockdown in the Control Room doesn't affect that."

You and Penny look at one another. "So we can escape now? Really?"

"You bet." He doesn't look very happy. "I had hoped to stop the reactor, and maybe even... ahh, well there's nothing to be done now. You two better hurry up and get to the surface."

"You're not coming with us?" you ask.

He waves it off. "I'm going to try one last thing and see if I can bypass the computer. I'll be right behind you guys, I promise. Go, hurry!"

"You take Penny's hand. "Come on, let's go!"

Run for it *ON PAGE 62*

108

It feels like you're floating. Everything is bright, and you aren't sure if your eyes are open or closed.

Slowly, the light begins to fade. Your other senses come around too: you hear a weird static sound, and there's an acrid smell in the air. Like burning.

You open your eyes.

You're on the ground, staring at the ceiling. You groan and get to your feet.

The Control Room looks like a bomb went off. Half the desks are turned over, with computer equipment scattered everywhere. It looks like an angry mob came in, smashed the computers against the walls, and then ran off. Loose sheets of paper cover the floor. A small fire crackles in the corner, the smoldering remains of a swivel chair. What happened in here?

You turn your eyes to the particle accelerator. The glass has been completely smashed, such that the large loop tube is open to the Control Room. You walk over there, feet crunching on tiny squares of glass. The orb, you remember. The Causality Neutrino. It had become unstable. That's what caused this.

Your hand begins to tremble. You whip your head around, looking for other people. There's nobody in sight. What happened to everyone? Are they gone?

And more importantly: are you all alone?

A computerized voice in the ceiling suddenly says, "Fire detected. Initiating sprinkler system."

"No!" you blurt out, running over to the small fire. It's hardly anything, just a small flame on the leg of the swivel chair. You take off your lab coat and bat at it, smothering it. With a sigh of relief you see that the flame has gone out, leaving just a thin trail of smoke drifting into the air.

A piercing alarm sounds. With a hiss the sprinkler system comes on anyways.

"No!" you blurt out, holding your coat over your head to shield yourself from the water. It cascades down in a million heavy streams, soaking everything. It begins to pool on the floor, the sound incredibly loud, as if you're standing next to a waterfall. The voice in the ceiling announces something, but you can't make it out.

Finally the sprinklers cut off. You shake the water off your coat. It may have helped, but the room is still submerged in about three inches of water. It's like a bath tub.

You're wondering what to do next when you hear someone groan across the room.

What are you waiting for? See who it is *ON PAGE 112*

You type the command to open the core, and then press enter.

The text disappears from the screen, and all that remains is a blinking cursor. You wonder if anything is happening.

Abruptly, you find out. There's a rushing sound, like a bathtub faucet pouring free. On each of the three outer walls is a circular door, halfway between the catwalks and the floor. They open, and a bluish liquid pours out and onto the floor in three separate waterfalls.

"*You initiated the coolant dump too soon!*" Jay cries.

Penny looks horrified. "What did you do?"

"I thought that was the next step!"

Liquid pours into the room, flooding the floor. The electronics down there begin shorting out, sending arcs of electricity into the air.

"*You have to get to the door,*" Jay says, sounding hurried. "*If you don't get there within two minutes...*"

"We can't!" Penny exclaims. "The floor is flooding!"

Helplessly, you watch as the liquid slowly rises. The core begins to groan as the pressure inside grows. You hope in vain that the coolant can do some of its job on the outside of the core, but it quickly becomes apparently that's not the case.

Penny sits on the catwalk and pulls her knees up to her chin. You can't even look at her. You were in charge, you had the sequence, and you entered the wrong one. This is a lousy way of reaching...

THE END

110

Penny's idea sounds best. You bob your head and say, "Yeah, let's distract it. Good thinking."

Penny beams.

"It's important that we choose the right item," Jay begins to lecture, but you've already found what you want. There's a flat slab of metal the size of a frisbee.

You flick it sideways and it spins through the air. You aimed to the right of the Phase Being, but it must have heard you because it whirls around with impossible reflexes. Its club of a hand snatches the metal out of the air.

The metal slab goes *through* the Phase Being, its iron atoms stripped away and sent hurtling through time. The result is the slab being split in half, each piece falling to the ground leaving a trail of strange glowing light. They clatter against the wall.

The Phase Being looks down at the metal, then back up at you.

"You have to be careful with what it touches," Jay says. "It's a good thing that slab was mostly iron. If you threw something with more complex elements we could have had a real explosion on our hands!"

"We have bigger problems," Penny says.

She's right. The Phase Being takes one cautious step toward you, as if walking on its legs for the first time. Then it takes another step.

"There's no way around it," you say. "Quick, to the backup reactor!"

Make a getaway *ON PAGE 61*

"Sure, we'll try the vents," you say. "Hopefully to Phase Beings can bother us in there." Penny removes the metal grate and you crawl into the dark tunnel, ignoring the spiderwebs and rat droppings brushing against your fingers.

You pass a vent that shows the inside of the Physics Room. There's a four-way intersection ahead. You picture the map of the laboratory in your head, imagining where the Maintenance Room is. "It's this way," you say.

The shaft veers to the right at an angle before continuing straight again. Any minute you should be above the Maintenance Room.

There: a grate up ahead, with a diagonal beam of light illuminating the air vent. You bang your way down toward it, excited.

"Is that it?" Penny asks.

You squint into the room. It's dark, and you can't see much of anything. "I can't tell. We need to get down in there and hope the lights work."

The grate flies away under your heel. You swing your legs into open air, then slide off the edge, twisting and grabbing the vent with your fingertips. You're hanging in the air. It's difficult to tell in the dark but you think you're not far above the ground.

You let go. There's a agonizingly long drop through the air–which is probably only half a second–before your feet strike the ground. You bend your knees, softening the landing. There's a weird smell in the air. "Come on down, it's not that far! Don't be afraid."

Before you can finish the sentence, there's a rush of air in front of you as Penny lands. It feels like she's grinning in the darkness.

You feel your way until you reach a wall, and then what seems like a door. You touch the wall along the frame until you find the light switch. The main overhead lights don't come on, but thankfully the emergency lights set in the wall do, bathing the room in red light.

Rows of cages line the wall, none of them larger than a television set. You realize what the smell before was: animal droppings. "We went too far. We're in the Animal Enclosure."

Check the room out by *TURNING TO PAGE 35*

112

You run to the corner, where a flat piece of ceiling tile is covering up what is now obviously a body. You pull the tile and other debris off and help the man up.

He's one of the physicists, with a white lab coat over a dress shirt and slacks. His straight hair is thick but mostly grey. He teeters where he stands, leaning on you for support.

"Hey, are you okay?" you ask. "Let's find somewhere for you to sit down."

The man looks around the room before his eyes latch onto you. He squints at you and appears dizzy. "I'm... uhh... I think I'm okay."

"What's your name?"

He blinks at you a few times, confused. "I am... uhh..." He pats his chest, looks down at himself. He searches all around. "My name tag. Where is..."

Oh man. This guy must have a concussion or something if he needs his name tag to remember his name. "Let's get you into a chair," you say, taking his arm.

He shakes his head and some clarity returns to his eyes. "Sorry, I'm just... disoriented. Call me Jay."

"Just Jay? Not 'Doctor' something?"

"Oh, I'm a doctor," he said. "But I hate titles. Too informal."

"Well, it's nice to meet you, Jay." You introduce yourself and shake his hand. He eyes you carefully, sizing you up, so you add, "I'm an intern here."

"Yes. I can see that." His mouth hangs open slightly while he looks around again. "Well this certainly went poorly, didn't it?"

"It sure did." You can feel a lump in the back of your throat as you think of your one job during the test: monitoring the reactor drainage. "And I think I know what caused this."

"Oh, I know exactly what happened too," Jay says.

"You do?"

He nods. "Of course I do. The Causality Neutrino."

You say, "Is that what that blue orb was?"

"Yes, the blue orb, of course. I remember now, it seemed so long ago..." He stares off into the distance for a moment, and you think you're about to lose him, until he continues. "The Causality Neutrino was created, just as the test intended. However, as many physicists predicted–" the way he says that makes it clear he means himself, "–it was too unstable for this laboratory to contain. It caused a rip in space-time."

"It did what now?" you ask.

He puts a hand on your shoulder. "Young mister Heller, let me explain to you how things work. Everything in the universe is made up of atoms."

You nod. "Everyone knows that."

"Well," he continues, "what are atoms made of? Protons, neutrons, and electrons. And that's it, right?"

"Right."

He jabs you in the chest with a bony finger. "Wrong! There's another subatomic particle called the Causality Neutrino. You see, protons, neutrons, and electrons all control where an atom is in space. But what about where it is in *time*?"

"Time?"

"Yes, time! What else? Objects don't just exist in three dimensions: they need a forth dimension, time, to pinpoint *when* they are. Think of it like a passenger jet."

"Okay." You don't see what this has to do with anything.

"You get the coordinates for a passenger jet, which tell you its location. But a moment later, it's in an entirely new location, because it's moving extremely fast! And an eye-blink later it's even farther away! That's because it's position in *time* has changed, young mister Heller."

"Ohh. Sort of like a clock."

He jabs his finger into the air. "Exactly! The Causality Neutrino is like a clock for atoms, to tell them *when* they are."

Pieces are starting to come together in your head. "So, we were able to create a Causality Neutrino here at the Heidelberg Laboratory?"

"It appears so."

"It went unstable," you say. "It was crackling with light, and sucking people and things into it... what happened to them? Where did they go?"

He leans down close, until his nose is practically touching yours. "Not *where* are they, young mister Heller. *When* are they!"

What? Figure out what's up *BACK ON PAGE 88*

114

You type the command to disable the safety system, and then press enter.

A motherly voice comes out of the terminal: "Safety systems: disabled."

"*Nice job there,*" Jay says. "*I remember now. Disabling the safety system is the first step, because otherwise it will kick-in and stop what you're doing.*"

"Nice going!" Penny says.

The options available on the screen are:

```
SELECT CORE FUNCTION
- FULL COOLANT DUMP
- EXTEND FLOOD TUBES
- OPEN CORE
- POWER UP BACKUP SYSTEM
```

"Do you remember the next step?" Penny asks. She's beginning to sound hopeful.

To perform a **Full Coolant Dump**, *GO TO PAGE 109*

To **Extend the Flood Tubes**, *GO TO PAGE 89*

To **Open the Core**, *GO TO PAGE 119*

To **Power Up the Backup System**, *GO TO PAGE 39*

You press enter.

There's a roaring sound, like a bathtub faucet pouring free. Bluish liquid rushes into the three coolant tubes, surging toward the core.

Penny pokes your arm. "What's that?" The computer screen is flashing:

```
ENTER CODE TO INITIATE SPECIAL SEQUENCE
```

"What code does it mean?" Penny asks.

Do you have a code to enter? If so, *GO TO THAT PAGE*
Otherwise, *HEAD TO PAGE 120*

116

You click on the word RACKET. There's a long pause on the screen, and the click of the computer's hard drive.

```
          INCORRECT INPUT
    CORRECT CHARACTER MATCH: 0
      SYSTEM LOCKDOWN: ACTIVE
      SYSTEM LOCKDOWN: ACTIVE
      SYSTEM LOCKDOWN: ACTIVE
```

"NO!" you and Penny cry out at the same time.

Jay slumps his head. "That was unfortunate."

"What are we going to do, Jay?"

"Well. There's good news, and bad news. The bad news is that the system is completely locked out, so we have no way of knowing if the core reactor is going to meltdown any time soon."

"And the good?"

"The good news is that by you two bringing up the network, the Decontamination Chamber is active. The system lockdown in the Control Room doesn't affect that."

You and Penny look at one another. "So we can get out of here? Really?"

"Uh huh." He doesn't look very happy. "I had hoped to stop the reactor, and maybe even... ahh, well there's nothing to be done now. You two better hurry up and get to the surface."

"You're not coming with us?" you ask.

He waves it off. "I'm going to try one last thing and see if I can bypass the computer. I'll be right behind you guys, I promise. Go, hurry!"

You take Penny's hand. "Come on, let's go!"

Make a getaway *ON PAGE 62*

"Maintenance Room #3 is as good a guess as any," you suggest.

Jay points to the wall. There's a square metal grate screwed into the wall at the corners. "You guys should take the air ventilation shaft. It will be quicker than walking."

Penny smirks. "The air vents? Seriously?"

Jay shrugs. "Why not? It worked in Die Hard. Come on, in you go."

You remove the screws and the grating. It's just big enough for you guys to crawl inside. "Just head in that general direction," Jay suggests, pointing. "You should reach the maintenance room at the end."

You lead the way, shimmying on all fours. The air shaft goes for about ten feet before splitting off. You pick the direction toward the third maintenance room.

Your wrists and knees make an awful lot of noise, banging hollowly on the metal as you move through the facility. There are grates spaced every ten feet or so, which provide enough light for you to see where you're going. You ignore the spiderwebs and piles of rat droppings that constantly brush against your arms.

The first ten grates you peer into don't look like the Maintenance Room. You pass the Recreation Room, one of the bathrooms, the Kitchen. Finally you come to a grate looking into a space that is identical to the first Maintenance Room. This has to be it!

Since it's screwed from the other side, you kick the grate with your foot until it flies off, banging onto the floor below. It's not very far, about a fifteen foot drop. You and Penny peer into the room together.

"I can't see anything from up here," she says.

"Me neither. We need to drop down inside."

You don't want Penny to think you're scared, so you swing your legs over. You're about to drop down into the room when she says, "WAIT!"

The yell almost causes you to fall. You regain your balance and ask "What?"

She points. "That dial says: **O2 Percentage**. Doesn't that mean oxygen?"

You sigh. "You're right. It does. We came the wrong way."

She playfully smacks you on the shoulder. "Then it's a good thing I stopped you from jumping, huh?"

If you think Maintenance Room #1 is right, *CRAWL TO PAGE 54*
Or, give Maintenance Room #2 a try *ON PAGE 72*

118

You hurry back to the Control Room. Jay is seated at one of the computer desks.

"Hey! We were able to–"

"Yeah yeah yeah," Jay says with a wave of a hand. "Computers came right up when you did. Good job. But now we've got a new problem. The system has a master password needed after a reboot."

"Is that bad? Don't you know it?"

"Only Kessler would know the password," Jay says. His eyes fall on Penny. "You wouldn't happen to know it, would you?"

She shrugs.

"Well, then we're just going to have to hack into it. Unfortunately, that means making some guesses. Take a look at this, young mister Heller."

The screen has a lot of green code, with the occasional word visible. Along the bottom of the screen are five words:

POURED BEHEAD THREAD SHREWD RACKET

"These are the possible passwords stored in the computer's memory," Jay says. He clicks on POURED and a new text clicks into place on the screen one letter at a time:

INCORRECT INPUT
CORRECT CHARACTER MATCH: 1
SYSTEM LOCKDOWN IN: TWO ATTEMPTS

"Character match is how many letters our guess has in common with the correct password," Jay explains. "Each time we guess, it'll tell us that. But we only have two more guesses before the system locks us out."

"But out of the remaining possibilities, they *all* have one letter in common," you say, exasperated. "POURED and BEHEAD share the last letter. POURED and RACKET share the second to last. How will we know?"

"Better guess another one then," Jay says.

Penny crowds next to the computer. "I'm usually good at these. Let's see..."

To guess **BEHEAD**, *GO TO PAGE 19*
To guess **THREAD**, *HEAD TO PAGE 33*
To guess **SHREWD**, *TRY PAGE 151*
To guess **RACKET**, *OPEN PAGE 73*

THE STRANGE PHYSICS OF THE HEIDELBERG LABORATORY

You type the command to open the core, and then press enter.

The text disappears from the screen, and all that remains is a blinking cursor. You wonder if anything is happening.

From the speaker in your suit, you hear Jay gasp. "*Did you just open the core?*"

"Yeah, it was the–"

"*You have made a very grave mistake!*" Jay shouts. "*Ohh. Without the flood tubes extended, the valves...*"

Sirens go off in the core room, and alarms flash red, spinning like police lights. You grip the catwalk railing and peer down at the core, where valves in the outer shell are beginning to open.

"*The radiation will be terrible. Get away! Quickly, get away!*"

You stare as the valve opens completely, and a new type of green glow shines out. Penny tugs on your arm.

"Come on! Let's *go.*"

She pulls you away and you bang down the catwalk.

"*It's too late,*" Jay bemoans. "*Now that the core is exposed, I can't open the blast doors for you!*"

The alarms grow louder as you slow to a stop. There's no point in even going down the ladder. You're doomed.

You turn and face the core. A strange glowing steam is drifting out. It looks almost peaceful... if it weren't, you know, radioactive.

You feel bad for failing. You feel even worse for Penny. She came up here to help you, and you let her down. For although you're fine for the time being, you have reached...

THE END

120

"I don't know what it means," you say.

"*You didn't find any special code along the way?*" Jay asks. "*Are you certain?*"

"Yep. Sorry, but we didn't."

Jay sounds disappointed, but quickly recovers. "*That's okay. For now, enjoy the show! You might want to take a step back, though. Just to be safe.*"

Coolant rushes into the core from the three tubes. Steam hisses out of every bolt and panel on the outside of the core, with sounds in every conceivable pitch. It doesn't feel safe there at all.

But slowly, *very* slowly, the steam begins to slow. Not only that, but the color coming from the core begins to change. It began as a neon green glow, then changes into the green of summer grass. The light continues weakening until there's almost nothing coming out at all.

You and Penny look at one another. Is that it?

"*You did it!*" Jay yells into your ears, practically deafening. "*Get back here so we can celebrate!*"

You retrace your steps, climbing down the ladder even more carefully than before. The blast door opens as you approach, and you jump out eagerly.

As soon as it closes behind you, Penny begins taking off her suit, clutching your shoulder for stability. Then she helps you remove yours.

"It feels great to have that off," she says.

"Yeah. Talk about claustrophobic."

Jay is standing in the Control Room with a wide smile on his face. "The computer has verified everything. Internal core pressure has fallen to 20 percent. Free electrons are dropping. The core is stable!"

You take a look at the computer. Sure enough, the bars that were climbing dangerously high earlier are now steadily dropping. The backup reactor is running smoothly, enough to power the entire facility.

Penny frowns. "Where are all the other scientists, though? Are they still stuck in time?"

Jay's smile wavers. "Yes. Well. We are not sure at this point. We will need to get a full team in here to check things out. It's possible they will become unstuck naturally, over time. Causality Neutrinos have a way of finding their way back to their proper atoms, eventually. But that may be a long time. Hopefully we can figure out a way to return them to normal."

You put a comforting hand on Penny's shoulder. "I'm sure your father is okay. Doctor Kessler is a smart man."

Without warning, she wraps her arms around you in a tight hug. You pat her back and tell her it's going to be okay.

"It's time for you two to get out of here," Jay says when the hug ends. "There are probably search and rescue teams on the surface preparing to come inside."

Penny smiles at him. "Thank you for helping us through everything. Even though your memory was full of holes, we couldn't have done it without you.

She moves to hug him, but Jay takes a step back and holds up his hands. "We, uhh, actually shouldn't hug just yet. You might be *slightly* radioactive after being inside the core, even with the suits on. No no, there's nothing to worry about, you just need to go through the Decontamination Chamber. Then you'll be good as new. I'll hug you when I join you later."

"You're not coming with us?" you ask.

"Not just yet. I want to run a few more diagnostics, double check a few things." His eyes fall on the CS Rifle. "Say, leave the rifle here, would you? Just in case."

Penny hands it over to him. You notice that he's careful not to touch her hand as he takes it.

"Now get going," he says with a departing smile. "I'll be up there soon. I promise."

You give him a final grateful smile and leave the Control Room.

You take your time walking through the hall to the Decontamination Chamber. The barrier looms above you, a massive blast door made of thick steel, designed to withstand a meltdown. Thankfully that's not needed, now. The control panel on its surface glows with electricity. You punch in a few keys and, with a loud groan, it opens.

Inside, you're blasted with powerful jets of hot air from all sides. The normally inconvenient process is pure joy, now. The system confirms you're clean and the door to the lobby opens.

The elevator car takes forever to descend, but finally it reaches your level, opening with a polite ding.

The ride up is just as long. After several minutes the doors open on the surface. The frigid air of the Alps buffets you in the face as you jump out of the car.

There are people waiting. A *lot* of people.

Face the crowd *ON PAGE 142*

122

"Well, I know that the copper wire is the *ground*," you say. "So it's safe."

"Are you certain?" Jay asks.

"Uh huh. Positive." To show your certainty, you jump into the puddle with the copper wire. There's a small splash, and then you stand there, frozen.

You turn back to Jay. "Told ya!"

Jay smiles. "You're pretty smart." He follows you through the puddle to the other side.

You reach the end of the room, where the door leads to the hallway toward the Particle Beam staging area. Something out of the corner of your eye catches your attention. It's the strangest visual sensation you've ever seen. The air seems to warp, the way the desert heat drifts off the ground in waves, distorting everything behind. Then the strange object begins to materialize, thickening into mist, then into some strange form of light. It's vaguely human-shaped, but made of what look like shards of light, angular and sharp, like chunks of jagged glass swirling in a small tornado.

"Ohh," Jay says, "I was hoping we wouldn't see this. That's a Phase Being."

"A *what?*"

"It's complicated," Jay says. "Now, we have a few options..."

You can avoid it by *GOING TO PAGE 20*

Or, if you have the CS Rifle, you can shoot it *ON PAGE 58*

"You wanted us to do that?" Penny asks. "Then why didn't you say so?"

"*Well... I'll explain that later, my dear Penny.*" There's a weird amount of affection in his voice. "*The Causality Protocol will use the CS Rifle to send an Electromagnetic Pulse throughout the facility. It will instantly fix all renegade Causality Neutrinos within a ten kilometer radius!*"

"You mean it will save all of the Phase Beings?"

Jay says, "*Precisely! You have done a wonderful job. Now enjoy the view of the Causality Protocol. It should be quite beautiful from there. And don't worry, it's perfectly safe for you two.*"

Penny puts her hands on the railing to watch as a robotic arm extends from the ceiling and picks up the CS Rifle.

"*Young mister Heller? Can you hear me?*"

"Of course I can, Jay."

There's a conspiratory tone to his voice. "*Okay, good. I am only speaking to you, now. Our dear Penny cannot hear us.*"

You frown. "Why? What's wrong? Are we really in danger here? Do we need to leave?"

Jay laughs. "*No, no, nothing like that. There's something I wanted to tell you, and only you. Turn to your left. Can you see me?*"

It takes you a moment, but you spot him: near the top of the wall, on the other side of a pane of glass. He's in one of the ancillary rooms overlooking the core reactor. He waves.

"*When you leave here, and return to the surface and tell everyone what happened, nobody will know who I am. They will say that no one named Jay works in the laboratory. And, frankly, they will be right.*"

"Are you saying you don't work here? You're not a physicist?"

"*Oh I'm definitely a physicist. And technically I do work here at the Heidelberg Physics Laboratory. Just... not in this part of time.*"

"I don't understand," you admit.

"*After everything you've seen, hopefully this doesn't come as a shock to you. Young mister Heller, I'm not from the same time as you and Penny. I'm from the year 2036.*"

124

You open your mouth but have no idea what to say to that.

"*When the Causality Neutrino became unstable, it disrupted the area around the Heidelberg Laboratory not just today, but in the future and the past.*"

"Right, which is why we've been seeing Phase Beings from other places in time," you say carefully. "But you don't look like a Phase Being. You're totally normal."

"*Yes, and I suspect I know the reason for that. Have you noticed how I have been extremely careful not to make physical contact with you or Penny?*"

You think back and realize he's right. He's been avoiding any handshakes, hugs, and high-fives throughout the day. The closest he's come to touching you was handing over the CS Rifle.

"*Firstly, I've been avoiding physical contact for fear that it would cause what happens with the other Phase Beings: disruption of your Causality Neutrinos, sending you spiraling through time. The second reason, however, is more theoretical. I've been specifically avoiding touching you, because I fear doing so would rip an entire hole in space-time through which all matter would be destroyed. I told you my name is Jay, but that is not entirely true. J is the first letter of my name, which I gave you because I could not tell you my true name. My name is... Jeremy Heller.*"

You nearly fall off the catwalk. You grab the railing to steady yourself, and Penny gives you a curious look.

You turn away from her so she can't see you talking inside your suit. "Pardon me?"

"*My name is Jeremy Heller. I am you, from the year 2036!*"

You stare across the room at the window where he is. His hair is much greyer than yours, but it has the same straight consistency. And his face *does* seem similar, you guess. Another thought creeps into your head. "Young mister Heller... you've been calling me young mister Heller all day! Because I really am the young version of you!"

Jay laughs. "*Yes, I felt weird calling you Jeremy. I was afraid my nickname for you would be too obvious, but I suppose it was fine. Anyways, when the Causality Neutrino went haywire during the test, and I suddenly appeared in the Control Room two decades in the past, I didn't understand what happened. But I believe being near you, my former self, somehow stabilized my own atoms. It didn't stabilize them completely, and if I touched either you or Penny things would really become chaotic, but it stabilized me enough to appear normal and touch regular objects. And, my presence near you kept you from being hurtled through time as well! We balanced each other out, young mister Heller, in a strange way.*"

"But if you knew all of this," you say, "why didn't you tell us? Why did we have to run all around the facility searching for the abort sequence if you knew it all along!"

"*Well, that's the thing about time travel,*" Jay muses. "*If I outright intervened, instead of allowing you to make the decisions for yourself, it could have had wide-reaching effects on the future. So I did my best to nudge you along the way, but all decisions and information gathering had to be done by you and Penny.*"

Before you, the coolant continues dumping into the core, and slowly the glow emanating from it begins to lessen. It goes from neon, to the color of summer grass, to a rich, deep green. Above the core, the robotic arm maneuvers the CS Rifle until it's pointing straight down into the core itself. Next to you, in a pleasant sounding motherly voice, the computer announces: "Beginning Emergency Causality Protocol."

A beam shoots from the CS Rifle; it's one continuous laser, instead of just a single shot. Energy pulses through the beam and into the center of the core. A strange bubble begins to grow from the core, expanding outward like a balloon.

"So this Causality Protocol is going to send you back to the year 2036?" you ask.

126

From the window across the room, Jay nods. "*It sure will. If you hadn't been able to find the special code, I would have probably shot myself with the Causality Rifle to send me back. But it's better this way, because now you'll save everyone else in the facility! As soon as that bubble expands and passes through the facility, all the physicists and engineers and workers will pop back into the correct time.*"

You watch as the bubble continues growing, a few feet at a time. Penny points and makes an excited face.

"I understand how everyone became displaced in time," you say. "And I understand how you, specifically, remained relatively stable because you were near another version of yourself–me, that is. But there's one thing I don't understand at all."

"*Yes?*"

"Penny Kessler. She's the only other one who wasn't catapulted into another time. And I *know* she's not a stable Phase Being, because she's touched my arm and hugged me several times now. So why was she immune from the Causality Neutrino's disruption? It doesn't make any sense at all."

Jay waits several seconds before answering. "*Well. I have a theory on that, but it's not as scientific as the other explanations.*"

"Everything else you've said has been correct, so I'm all ears."

"*Penny Kessler remained stable in this timeline because of her close relationship to you–that is to say, her close relationship with us.*"

"What do you mean? I just met her this morning. I barely know her!"

"*Yes, that is true. However, in the future, you and Penny have a far more thorough acquaintance.*"

You look at Penny. She's still watching the bubble expanding from the core. "Jay, are you saying that in the future you... I mean me... do Penny and I become more than just friends?"

"*Something like that.*" Across the room a big grin splits Jay's face.

"What do you mean?" You feel a flurry of nervousness in your stomach. "Tell me!"

"*Let's just say yours and Penny's futures are irreparably bound together. And don't worry, Doctor Kessler warms up to you eventually. In fact, running the emergency abort sequence and saving the Heidelberg Laboratory is one of the things that finally gets him to like you. Oh, and go easy on him in the aftermath of the disaster. He was the one to overpower the Particle Beam, causing the unstable Causality Neutrino, which you'll soon discover, but he learns his lesson and is more careful in the future.*"

"Hey, you're not being very specific about me and Penny! Tell me more!"

"*I'm afraid I can't be too specific, or it might interfere with your futures. But I think you understand what I'm saying. You're a smart guy, after all!*" He chuckles at his own joke.

The bubble continues expanding until it approaches the catwalk. Penny takes a nervous step backwards but you put a hand on her arm.

"*Don't worry, Penny dear,*" Jay says, reenabling Penny's communication. "*The Causality bubble will not harm you. It might tickle, though. So don't fall!*"

You watch as the bubble drifts closer. You brace yourself as it nears, touching your face and hands. It passes through you like a cold wind, touching your skin as if you're not wearing any suit at all. It leaves a tingling sensation across your body.

"That was cool!" Penny exclaims.

"*Very cool,*" Jay says. "*Now, Penny, I'm afraid I need to leave now. I'm going to return to the surface, but I will meet up with you later. If you don't mind, I'm going to talk to Jeremy one last time, privately.*"

Penny spins around to watch the bubble continuing to spread. "Okay," she says, enraptured by it.

"*You will have to make something up about me,*" Jay says to you. "*You cannot tell her the truth, or it might scare her away. Do you understand?*"

You think she would handle the truth well enough–she's pretty level-headed–but you nod. "I understand. I'll tell her you were called away quickly to help with the clean-up of the facility."

"*That will work.*" The bubble is quickly nearing Jay's location up in the window. "*It's time for me to leave now. Oh, and one last thing.*"

"Yes?"

"*When you and Penny go skiing in 2024, avoid the slope with all the moguls. Those are the bumpy spots that are difficult to navigate. Trust me!*"

As he says that, the Causality bubble passes through the glass and into the room. Jay raises his hand in a final wave.

"*Goodbye, young mister Heller.*"

Jay looks blurry and bright, like a photograph out of focus. He begins to split apart into mist, first at his legs, then moving up his torso into his head and arms. You know it's his atoms being reset, their Causality Neutrinos returned to normalcy. Being thrust forward in time, back to the year 2036 where they belong. The atoms continue to dissipate into the air, into a cloud, then a mist, then nothing at all.

"Goodbye, Jay," you say.

Penny turns toward you. "Did you say something?" It looks like your communications are connected again.

"Nothing. Come on, let's get out of here."

You head down the ladder and across the room to the blast door. It's closed, and there's no control panel or anything to open it.

Penny presses the button to the PA next to the door. "Hey, Jay? Before you go, can you let us out of here?"

Jay's not there, though she doesn't know that. How are you going to get out? Are you stuck in the core?

But the PA crackles and someone answers. "Penny? Is that you?"

"Dad!" Penny cries out. "It's me! Jeremy and I are inside the reactor core."

"The core? Oh no. Oh nooo this is very bad, Penny, why did you..."

"It's fine, Doctor Kessler," you speak up. "We came in here to initiate the emergency reactor abort sequence."

"The sequence... how could you possibly..." He cuts off and you hear the sound of keys being typed. "Stand back. The blast door is going to open."

You do as your told. The huge locks disengage, and the door opens wide enough for the two of you to slip through. Penny runs down the hall, and you follow her into the Control Room.

Kessler is waiting on the other side, and wraps his daughter in a big hug. "Oh, Penny! My sweet Penny. I was so afraid you weren't safe."

Your mouth hangs open as you survey the room. Although it looks the same as before–debris everywhere, computers and desks damaged, with a thin layer of water on the ground from the sprinklers–now it's filled with all the physicists from before. Many of them are holding their heads, looking confused.

Doctor Almer, your boss, is sitting at the computer Jay was previously using. He says, "Doctor Kessler, he's right. They successfully entered the sequence!"

130

Penny lets go of her dad. "Jeremy did it, I just went in with him for support." She looks around the room. "Hey, where is..."

You realize she's wondering about Jay. You unzip your HAZMAT suit and quickly say, "He's gone now. He'll meet up with us later." You turn to Kessler. "Sir, you and the other physicists were stuck in time after the Causality Neutrino test. I gathered the six steps in the sequence and reset everything."

Kessler looks you up and down. "*You* did this? An intern?"

You nod.

"What an amazing feat! The emergency abort sequence has never been run in the history of the lab, and you carried it out and saved my daughter in the process. Doctor Almer, why is this young man just an intern?"

Almer looks embarrassed. "I don't know, sir."

Kessler puts a hand on your shoulder. "We're going to change that. We need more physicists like you, Jeremy. I want to hire you full-time. Your first duty will be to figure out how this mess happened!"

You remember what Jay–your future self–said: how Kessler was the one to overload the Particle Beam and cause the disaster in the first place. Awkwardly, you say, "Of course, I'll get to the bottom of it."

He leaves you then, and goes to examine some of the data on one of the computers.

Some fingers find your hand. You look down and see they're Penny's, wrapped in your own. "I think my dad likes you. And he doesn't like *anybody*." She's smiling happily at you.

You're not sure what to say. "Yeah, I guess you win a lot of friends when you save an entire physics laboratory from disaster."

She laughs a carefree laugh at your joke. "Are you hungry? You're coming to our house for dinner tonight. I insist. My mom makes the most *amazing* spaetzle. German noodles, cooked with butter. My dad usually hates when I bring boys over for dinner, but something tells me he'll be fine with you. So you'll come? To dinner?"

"Of course I will come to dinner!"

"Great. Then it's settled. I want to get out of this crazy laboratory, but I don't want to go alone. Will you take me up to the surface?"

You give her the most charming smile you can. "Penny, I'd love to escort you there."

"Hopefully we'll see Jay up above! I really liked him."

You walk toward the Decontamination Chamber, hand-in-hand. "Oh, don't worry. I'm sure you'll see Jay again in the future."

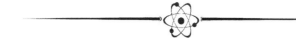

CONGRATULATIONS!
YOU HAVE REACHED THE ULTIMATE ENDING!

In recognition for taking up the gauntlet, let it be known to fellow adventurers that you are hereby granted the title of:

Causality Crusader!

You may go here: **www.ultimateendingbooks.com/extras.php** and enter code:

EZ68591

for tons of extras, and to print out your Ultimate Ending Book Four certificate!

And for a special sneak peek of Ultimate Ending Book 7, *TURN TO PAGE 153*

132

"...and unfortunately," Jay says, "we just don't have enough steps."

"Why not?" you ask. "We have time to look for them. I know we can!"

Jay says, "It's too risky. We need at least ten minutes to get inside the core and run the sequence. That leaves twenty minutes to scour the entire facility for the steps we're missing."

"Twenty minutes seems like enough to..." Penny says.

"It's just not enough time. Don't you understand that? It's not enough time!"

You fumble around for an excuse. "Can we guess the missing sequences? We have to try!"

Jay rolls away from the computer. "Entering the sequence wrong will cause it to meltdown early. You two have to get out of here. *Now.* Get to the surface, and I'll do what I can to delay the meltdown. Leave the CS Rifle here. Go, come on! GO!"

His anger shocks you into movement. You give Jay one last look–he seems strangely sad–before dropping the CS Rifle on the desk.

You sprint through the hall toward the Decontamination Chamber. The barrier looms above you, a massive blast door made of thick steel, designed to withstand a meltdown. The control panel on its surface glows with electricity. You punch in a few keys and, with a loud groan, it opens.

Inside, you're blasted with powerful jets of hot air from all sides. The normally inconvenient process is pure joy, now. The system confirms you're clean and the door to the lobby opens.

You rush to the elevator door to press the button. The elevator car takes forever to descend, but finally it reaches your level, opening with a polite ding.

The ride up is just as long. After several minutes the doors open on the surface. The frigid air of the Alps buffets you in the face as you jump out of the car.

And into an enormous crowd of armed people.

See what's going on by *HEADING TO PAGE 134*

You spin around to face the glass wall, but you already know what you're going to see. The air distorts and twists, and a Phase Being appears in front of the window.

"That's what happens when a person gets stuck in time," Jay says. "They're simultaneously existing in multiple points in time. That's why we can't see them clearly."

"That's a *person*?" Penny looks horrified. "Could that be my father?"

The Phase Being cocks its head at you.

You nod. "Maybe. Which is why we need to help them."

The other Phase Being seemed unable to move, but this one takes a slow step forward. Then, without warning, it dives across the room. Right at Penny!

If you have the CS Rifle, shoot it *ON PAGE 140*

Otherwise, grab Penny and pull her away *ON PAGE 71*

134

The men are uniformed, with rifles held across their chests and SWAT style helmets covering their heads. For a moment they're surprised by your appearance. Then they aimed their guns at you. They begin shouting in accented French.

You raise your hands. There's not much else for you to do. Behind them on the mountain top sit two helicopters, with men unloading gear from inside. In the distance you see three more approaching your location. Wow, this is a big deal! It's like a military invasion.

"Penny? Penny!" Someone pushes through the ring of SWAT members. It's Penny's dad, Doctor Kessler. He runs forward and embraces her. "Oh, Penny. I thought you were gone!"

She frowns and pushes him away. "How did you get up here? You left me down there!"

"Sweetie, I don't know what happened." He looks confused. "The Causality Neutrino went haywire, there were papers and debris flying in all directions... it felt like I was flying through the air, even though my feet stayed planted on the ground. Then suddenly... I appeared here. Up on the surface. We called the emergency response team, but everything was locked down. Even the elevator, until just a few minutes ago."

"The Causality Neutrino displaced you," you say. "You were stuck in time."

Kessler sees you for the first time. "Stuck in time? Who are you?"

"This is the man who *saved* me," Penny says. "His name is Jeremy Heller."

"He's just an intern," Kessler says dismissively. "He doesn't know what he's talking about."

"Sure I do. Jay told me..."

You trail off as another rumble shakes the mountain. Up high, with the other mountain peaks in the distance and the valley below, it gives you the feeling of being near a volcano when it erupts. The shaking goes on for several seconds, and knocks a few people to their knees.

Finally it stops. "I think that was the big one," Penny says.

"Jay said we had lots of time left," you say. "He was down there!"

"Who is Jay? What's his last name?" Kessler asks.

"Jay, one of the physicists. I don't know his last name. He stayed down there to try to stop the core from melting down. We were collecting parts of the shutdown sequence..."

Kessler scrunches his face up. "And did you succeed? The sequence is printed in manuals all over the facility!"

"I... we tried, but... there was so much damage and debris everywhere it was tough to find..."

Medics appear and wrap blankets around you and Penny. You're given cups of warm broth too. Kessler goes over to a makeshift radio system that has been erected in the snow and shouts orders into the receiver. A while later he returns.

"Well," Kessler says. "The facility is indeed lost."

You and Penny slump your heads. "So did Jay..."

"There is no 'Jay' that works here," Kessler interrupts. "I know everyone in the facility. Regardless..." He sighs. "You've brought my precious daughter out in one piece. For that, I am eternally grateful. You have done well, Jeremy Heller."

You try to protest more, but someone calls Kessler over to the elevator, and he descends into the Laboratory. You look at Penny. "I didn't imagine Jay, did I?"

She shrugs. "Nope, he was definitely there. Hey, why didn't we get stuck in time like the others? It seems like a strange coincidence that hundreds of people disappeared except you, me, and Jay."

Huh, that *is* strange. "I don't know. I'm sure they'll figure it out in the coming days."

She rests her head on your shoulder. "Do you have a place to stay?"

Her head feels warm on your shoulder. "I'm renting a room from an old woman in town. It's above a restaurant, so it's loud, but I don't mind."

"Why don't you come home with me and dad tonight? My mom makes great spaetzle."

"What's that?"

"German noodles. They're delicious! I won't take no for an answer. It's settled, you'll come get a warm meal with us. You deserve it." She lifts her head and looks at you. "You *saved* me. I'll never forget that."

There's a warmth in her eyes that relieves you of all the fears of the day. There's something special about Penny, you can feel it. It's as if you've known her your entire life. "Yeah. I'd like that."

She smiles, and you feel happy to have reached...

THE END

136

You type the command to open the core, and then press enter.

The text disappears from the screen, and all that remains is a blinking cursor. You wonder if anything is happening.

Abruptly, you find out. There's a rushing sound, like a bathtub faucet pouring free. Bluish liquid rushes into the three coolant tubes, surging toward the core. But when they reach the outer shell, they begin spraying out the side of the valve instead. The force is so strong that the tubes are pushed back with a groan of steel, and the coolant dumps straight down on the ground.

"*You initiated the coolant dump too soon!*" Jay cries. "*You were supposed to open the core first!*"

Penny looks horrified. "What did you do?"

"I thought that was the next step!"

Liquid pours into the room, flooding the floor. The electronics down there begin shorting out, sending arcs of electricity into the air.

"*You have to get to the door,*" Jay says, sounding hurried. "*If you don't get there within two minutes...*"

"We can't!" Penny exclaims. "The floor is flooding!"

Helplessly, you watch as the liquid slowly rises. The core begins to groan as the pressure inside grows. You hope in vain that the coolant can do some of its job on the outside of the core, but it quickly becomes apparently that's not the case.

Penny sits on the catwalk and pulls her knees up to her chin. You can't even look at her. You were in charge, you had the sequence, and you entered the wrong one. This is a lousy way of reaching...

THE END

You finish making your way to the Control Room. It looks like a tornado ran through the room, just the way you left it.

"Oh my gosh," Penny says, sloshing through the few inches of water. "And I thought the Observation Lounge was bad!"

Jay nods. "Yeah, looks like the Causality Neutrino really did a number during the test. I have some theories as to what went wrong."

You scratch the back of your head. "Actually... I think I know."

Jay smirks. "Go ahead."

"My job is to monitor the reactor power levels. Normally everything is fine, but today the power kept spiking. Something was drawing a *lot* of power from the reactor. More than normal."

"And we saw what that was," Jay comments. "Remember?"

You think back. "The Particle Beam staging room!"

Jay nods in confirmation.

"I don't understand," Penny says.

"It was before we reached the Observation Lounge," you say. "The Particle Beam, which creates the protons which are launched into the particle accelerator, was tampered with. Someone supercharged it to twice the recommended level!"

"Why is that bad?"

"Well," Jay says, gesturing to the destroyed room, "it's bad because that much power could create a very unstable Causality Neutrino."

"Oh."

"Oh indeed, my dear Penny. And that's not even the worst part."

"Wait, it's not?" you say.

"Of course not, young mister Heller. You should know what the bigger problem is."

You scrunch your forehead in thought. "I don't know."

"Think! You know this!"

"Look, it's tough to think right now," you say. "Just tell me so we can..."

"Is it the reactor?" Penny asks.

Jay snaps his finger. "Bingo. The reactor. It might have been..."

You finish his sentence. "...might have been damaged due to the extra load on it during the test. The reactor core could suffer a meltdown!"

That's bad. *FLIP TO PAGE 138*

138

"So it might have a meltdown," Penny says. "Can't you just turn it off?"

"Well, it's not that simple." Jay clasps his hands behind his back like a college professor. "You see, nuclear reactions are precarious things. Enriched uranium atoms become unstable and split, which in turn causes other uranium atoms to become unstable, and so on. We control this chain reaction by extending special rods into the nuclear reactor, which slow the reaction by absorbing all the extra electrons flying around."

"Then let's do that."

"*Unfortunately,*" Jay says, "if a reaction is too far along, with too many unstable uranium atoms inside, the chain reaction cannot be stopped. The core will get hotter, and the pressure greater, until it eventually explodes."

There's a short silence as the reality of that sinks in.

"Then what can we do?" Penny asks.

"Well, there's an emergency core shutdown sequence that we can follow to stop a meltdown," Jay says. "So it's good that we've already found some of the sequence. There are five steps altogether, so we'll need to find the others."

"Let's get looking!" you say.

"The core override sequence is just for emergencies, though. So before we do that, we need to confirm the core's status, and make sure it's actually going to meltdown." Jay points to the nearest computer. "But there's no way to verify with the computer network offline. We need to get it operational again."

"I don't know," you say. "The core could meltdown at any moment. Maybe we should evacuate the lab while we can."

"We *could* do that," Jay says, "if we were cowards."

"Hey, I'm just saying–"

"But it doesn't matter anyways," Jay mutters as he walks away, "because the computer system also controls the decontamination chamber. Currently it's locked tight. If the network is shutdown, so is our way out of the lab."

"Oh yeah, that's right." You glance at Penny and feel foolish for suggesting it. "I guess we need to get the network online, then. How do we do that?"

Jay stops by the wall, where a printed map of the Heisenberg Physics Laboratory is posted. "I'm glad you asked."

Review the map *ON PAGE 98*

The Kitchen is a long, narrow room with stainless steel surfaces all along both walls, with room to walk down the middle. An industrial style ventilation system hangs above eight stove burners on the left. The ovens are on the right, four of them in a row, large enough to cook a meal for an entire facility full of scientists, engineers, and workers. Everything is clean and pristine, except for a single mixing bowl on the near shelf. You look inside: someone was mixing cookie dough. They must have gotten stuck in time right in the middle of it. It's a grim reminder of the disaster with the Causality Neutrino test.

Penny senses your mood. Wordlessly, the two of you begin opening cabinets and searching drawers. You find lots of utensils, pots and pans and cutting boards. One shelf has a row of cookbooks. They're mostly in German, French, and Italian.

At the end of the room, taped to a refrigerator, is a handwritten note:

Jessica, I swear, if you leave your leftovers in the fridge over the weekend again I'm going to put a padlock on the door! This kitchen is for everyone. It's not your personal food hiding spot.

After that, you've reached the end of the room. You've found nothing.

The PA in the ceiling cuts on. "*Eight minutes. You guys have eight minutes left. Hope you're making progress!*"

"Where should we search next?" Penny asks.

There's a hall running toward the Sleeping Quarters, which also connects to the back of the two Bathrooms. Another door leads into the Supply Closet.

Check the Sleeping Quarters *ON PAGE 68*
Inspect the Bathrooms *ON PAGE 30*
Hurry to the Supply Closet *ON PAGE 45*

140

The Phase Being lunges. Moving with instinct, you pull the rifle from over your shoulder and squeeze the trigger without aiming.

The shot rings out in the Observation Lounge with a flash of light. The Phase Being freezes in mid-lunge as it's struck by the beam. The changing shapes that make up its body begin to flicker with color instead of just light, materializing into more solid forms. It spreads from the point where the beam struck, in the chest and down the legs, up into the shoulders and into the arms and hands. For a brief instant in time you see its face: a woman with long blonde hair tied back in a ponytail.

And then with a *pop* she's gone.

Penny looks horrified. "I recognized her. That was Jessica. She's worked with my father for years. Did you... did she...?"

You quickly shake your head. "The CS Rifle fixes them, unsticking them from time."

"Then why did she disappear? Why isn't she here right now?"

"That means she came from another time," Jay explains. "The instability of the Causality Neutrino was so great that it affected not just the people in the Heidelberg Laboratory today, but all the people here in both the past and future!"

"The CS Rifle sent her back to the correct time for *her*," you add.

Penny says, "But if the Causality Neutrino affected all of the investors, and affected people in the future, why didn't it affect me? And why didn't it affect either of you?"

It's a good question you hadn't even considered. You glance at Jay.

"You are a very intelligent young woman," he says with a smile. "And that is a valid question. But the creation of this Causality Neutrino is too new of a scientific breakthrough. All we have are theories right now. I'm afraid I do not have an explanation."

"We'll just have to count ourselves as lucky," you say.

"Lucky indeed, young mister Heller. Let's get moving."

Head back to the Control Room and *FLIP TO PAGE 47*

You head down the corridor to another security door. After punching in the code, it opens into the Test Simulator. It's strange seeing the three projectors in the ceiling offline, even though the servers in the corner are still making noise.

Penny turns her attention to the two file cabinets against the wall. "I'll take the left cabinet, you take the right."

You get to work pulling open drawers and sifting through papers. Most of the information is printed in three-ring binders, and fortunately they're labeled. *Beam Focus Adjustment*, 422 pages long. *Small Loop Maintenance Cycle*, 244 pages. There's even a binder with instructions on what to do if someone fails to be properly cleaned in the Decontamination Chamber. 158 pages for that.

"Any luck?" you ask.

Penny shakes her head and stands. She begins to go through the second drawer.

It seems like they have a manual for everything in this place. You find one called *Core Drain Monitoring*, and for a moment your heart skips a beat, but a quick browse of the pages and you realize it's not the one. In fact, it's the manual on how to do *your* job.

The job you used to have, at least. You doubt it will matter soon.

You go through all the drawers before giving up. "Well this was a waste of time," you say.

Penny scratches the back of her head and looks at the floor.

"*Five minutes left,*" Jay calls on the PA. "*You've got five minutes until we absolutely need the code, or else we have to evacuate.*"

"Where to next?" Penny asks.

To explore the Animal Enclosure, *RUN TO PAGE 106*
To search Maintenance Room #2 again, *GO BACK TO PAGE 97*

THE STRANGE PHYSICS OF THE HEIDELBERG LABORATORY

142

The men are uniformed, with rifles held across their chests and SWAT style helmets covering their heads. For a moment they're surprised by your appearance. Then they aimed their guns at you. They begin shouting in accented French.

You raise your hands. There's not much else for you to do. Behind them on the mountain top sit two helicopters, with men unloading gear from inside. In the distance you see three more approaching your location. It's like a military invasion!

"Penny? Penny!" Someone pushes through the ring of SWAT members. It's Penny's dad, Doctor Kessler. He runs forward and embraces her. "Oh, Penny. I thought you were gone!"

At first she hugs him back and cries out with joy. Then she frowns and pushes him away. "How did you get up here? You left me down there!"

"Sweetie, I don't know what happened." He looks confused. "The Causality Neutrino went haywire, there were papers and debris flying in all directions... it felt like I was flying through the air, even though my feet stayed planted on the ground. Then suddenly... I appeared here. Up on the surface. We called the emergency response team, but everything was locked down. Even the elevator, until just a few minutes ago."

"The Causality Neutrino displaced you," you say. "You were stuck in time."

Kessler sees you for the first time. "Stuck in time? Who are you?"

"This is the man who *saved* me," Penny says. "His name is Jeremy Heller."

"He's just an intern," Kessler says dismissively. "He doesn't know what he's talking about."

"Sure I do. Jay told me..."

"Who is Jay? What's his last name?" Kessler asks.

"Jay, one of the physicists. I don't know his last name. He helped us collect the emergency core abort sequence."

Kessler's eyes widen. "The abort sequence... Did you succeed? Well?"

You try to remain humble, but a big smile invades your face. "We did. We ran the five steps inside the reactor core and stopped a meltdown." Penny bobs her head in agreement.

Kessler's mouth hangs open. "But... you are just an intern! How could you possibly accomplish that?"

Medics appear and wrap blankets around you and Penny.

"I told you. Jay helped us."

"There is no 'Jay' that works here. I know everyone in the facility." He smacks you on the shoulder. "Come on now. Is 'Jay' just a nickname for 'Jeremy'? You won't get in trouble. You saved the facility! Take the credit."

"But I'm telling you..."

"We need to give you more responsibilities here," Kessler continues. "As soon as the Laboratory is cleaned up I'm hiring you full-time. No more of this intern business. How does that sound?"

You try to protest more, but someone calls Kessler over to the elevator. They talk for a few minutes, and he descends into the Laboratory.

You look at Penny. "I didn't imagine Jay, did I?"

She shrugs. "Nope, he was definitely there. Hey, why didn't we get stuck in time like the others? It seems like a strange coincidence that hundreds of people disappeared except you, me, and Jay."

Huh, that *is* strange. "I don't know. I'm sure they'll figure it out in the coming days. Hopefully they'll be able to save all the other Phase Beings, too."

She rests her head on your shoulder. "Do you have a place to stay?"

Her head feels warm on your shoulder. "I'm renting a room from an old woman in town. It's above a restaurant, so it's loud, but I don't mind."

"Why don't you come home with me and dad tonight? My mom makes great spaetzle."

"What's that?"

"German noodles. They're delicious! I won't take no for an answer. It's settled, you'll come get a warm meal with us. You deserve it." She lifts her head and looks at you. "And not just for saving the Heisenberg Laboratory. You saved *me*. I'll never forget that, Jeremy Heller."

There's a warmth in her eyes that relieves you of all the fears of the day. There's something special about Penny, you can feel it. It's as if you've known her your entire life. "Yeah. I'd like that."

She smiles.

You're ushered onto a helicopter to be taken back to the city at the base of the mountain. Penny holds your hand the entire time. Despite the failed test, and despite all the trouble afterward, you decide it was a good day. You had an adventure. You got to use your knowledge of physics to save the day. And, most importantly to you just then, you've made a good friend in Penny. This is a pretty wonderful way to reach...

THE END

144

You type the command to extend the flood tubes, and then press enter.

There's a massive groan of machinery, coming from all directions. You realize the source: doors have opened on three walls, below you, halfway to the floor. Slowly, a few inches at a time, the flood tubes are being extended from each of the three coolant towers. They crane across the open space beneath you until they connect to valves on the outer surface of the core.

They make a *KA-CLUNK* sound as they connect to the core.

Jay says, "*You're doing great, young mister Heller. Everything looks good from the Control Room. Keep going!*"

The options available on the screen are:

```
SELECT CORE FUNCTION
- FULL COOLANT DUMP
- OPEN CORE
```

Penny grins like a fool. "You can do it Jeremy!"

To perform a **Full Coolant Dump,** *GO TO PAGE 136*
To **Open the Core,** *GO TO PAGE 148*

You move steadily, waiting until each body part has advanced before moving the next one. Right arm. Left leg. Left arm. Right leg. Slow and steady.

Your breathing sounds hollow and ragged inside the suit. It begins to fog up your faceplate. You take your hand off the ladder to try wiping it away, but it doesn't help much. There's nothing to do but continue.

Up you go, on and on, carefully avoiding looking down. You keep your eyes straight ahead, on the rungs in front of your face and the wall behind the ladder.

Soon it's obvious you're high in the air. You can *feel* the expanse of open air underneath you. It threatens to suck you back into it, falling to your doom. With each step you're terrified you will lose your grip and plummet.

But then you reach up and can't find the next rung. You tilt your head back and realize you've reached the top, where the end of the catwalk is. You pull yourself the rest of the way up, feet banging on the metal grate platform.

You help Penny up, then move along the catwalk toward the center of the room. Where the top of the core is.

"*Good job,*" Jay says in your ear. "*You should be able to access the administrator's terminal. Just press the spacebar.*"

The terminal is built low into a sort of table that stands up from the catwalks. To the right, on the other side of the railing, is the open top of the core, with dozens of long rods sticking inside. You turn back to the terminal and press the spacebar. Green text moves across the screen.

```
SELECT CORE FUNCTION
- FULL COOLANT DUMP
- DISABLE SAFETY SYSTEM
- EXTEND FLOOD TUBES
- OPEN CORE
- POWER UP BACKUP SYSTEM
```

"*Okay,*" Jay says. "*Do you remember the order you're supposed to run the sequence?*"

To perform a **Full Coolant Dump,** *GO TO PAGE 109*
To **Disable the Safety System,** *GO TO PAGE 114*
To **Extend the Flood Tubes,** *GO TO PAGE 89*
To **Open the Core,** *GO TO PAGE 119*
To **Power Up the Backup System,** *GO TO PAGE 46*

146

"It's the code I found in the bathroom," you say. You thumb the numbers into the keypad: **1 - 4 - 6.**

CODE ACCEPTED. PLEASE PLACE CS RIFLE IN PIVOT MOUNT

Penny unslings the CS Rifle from her shoulder. You didn't even realize she had it. "What's the pivot mount?"

Above the top of the core, where the dozens of rods are sticking out, a new pedestal rises into place next to the catwalk. There's an indentation in the metal the exact shape of the rifle.

You take it from Penny. "I guess we just put it in?"

The coolant is rushing into the core, and steam is hissing off at several random angles. You take a cautious step toward the edge, lean forward, and place the CS Rifle on the mount.

You quickly step back from the ledge as the pedestal extends back over the core. The computer types:

INITIATING EMERGENCY CAUSALITY PROTOCOL

"Were we supposed do that?" Penny asks.

"*As a matter of fact,*" Jay interrupts, "*that was the very thing I hoped you two would do.*"

Find out what he means *ON PAGE 123*

THE STRANGE PHYSICS OF THE HEIDELBERG LABORATORY

147

The Sleeping Quarters are like a military barracks. There's an aisle down the center of the room, with rows of bunk beds on either side. Personal lockers are mounted on the wall between the bunks. Long rugs cover the floor.

"Those lockers contain personal information," you tell Penny. "But, there might be technical info as well."

You split up to each cover half the room. The lockers have a small key-lock on them, but they're weak enough that you can pull it open with a little force.

The first locker belongs to a woman: there's a box of makeup, a contact lens case, and a photo of a family of three smiling at a camera. It's a sad reminder that many of the people from the facility are still stuck in time.

But there's no sequence. You move on to the next locker: this one has a chocolate protein bar, a stack of postcards, and a box of Q-tips.

"JEREMY!" Penny suddenly shouts.

You whirl to see a Phase Being striding across the room. It doesn't see you–it's too focused on Penny, trapped between two bunks.

Moving with instinct instead of thought, you fire the CS Rifle. The solid beam of white travels the distance instantaneously, striking the Phase Being square in the back.

There's a flashing like camera bulbs as it morphs and twists, gaining color and shape. You see the outline of a young woman with short red hair, wearing a lab coat, and then she blinks out of existence. The sheets on the beds nearby blow back from the energy release, and then everything is still.

You rush to where she just was, but it doesn't look like she dropped anything. Penny meets you there and smiles sheepishly. "Thank you for saving me."

You blush. "Sure. You would've done the same for me, right?"

Before she can answer, the PA cuts on. "*Eight minutes. You guys have eight minutes left. Hope you're making progress!*"

"There's nothing in here," Penny tells you. "It's all just personal stuff."

There's a hall running toward the Kitchen, which also connects to the back of the two Bathrooms. Another door leads into the Supply Closet. Where to?

Check the Kitchen *ON PAGE 57*
Inspect the Bathrooms *ON PAGE 30*
Hurry to the Supply Closet *ON PAGE 45*

148

You type the command to open the core. You hear the sound of machinery, like when the doors that extended the flood tubes opened. You realize you can't see it because it's happening where the tubes are connected to the core valves.

Abruptly the noise stops. "*The core is open!*" Jay shouts. "*You're almost there! Finish the abort sequence! Hurry!*"

There's only one command left on the screen now:

```
SELECT CORE FUNCTION
- FULL COOLANT DUMP
```

You type in the command, but stop right before pressing enter. "Want to do the honors?"

Penny frowns. "Seriously?"

"Sure. Why not?"

She grabs your hand. "Let's do it together."

Perform the **Full Coolant Dump** *ON PAGE 115*

"Let's check the Bathrooms," you decide. "I'll search the men's room, you search the women's."

You split up. The men's restroom has been visited by the Causality Neutrino: a sphere-shaped hole has been cut out of one of the stalls, leaving the door hanging on a single hinge. Water trickles onto the floor.

It's immediately obvious this was a mistake. Nothing would be in here. You begin to turn around to go get Penny–

You stop. Taped to the mirror above the sink is a slip of paper. You tear it off and read:

NOT ONLY IS IT POSSIBLE TO RESET THE CAUSALITY NEUTRINOS IN ALL ATOMS WITHIN THE FACILITY, BUT IT IS HIGHLY RECOMMENDED FOLLOWING A CATASTROPHIC DISASTER. BY ENTERING CODE 1-4-6 INTO THE CORE REACTOR AS THE SIXTH STEP IN THE ABORT SEQUENCE, A CAUSALITY SHOCKWAVE WILL EMANATE FROM THE REACTOR. THIS WILL SERVE TO...

Sixth step? Jay said there were only five! You take the paper and rush into the women's room to find Penny.

She smiles at you as you enter. "*Excuse me*, but this is the ladies room. Do you belong in here?"

You thrust the paper at her. She takes it and reads, her eyes growing wider and wider. "But Jay said..."

"...there were only five steps, yeah. This doesn't make sense to me, either."

Somewhere out in the hall, the PA comes alive. Jay's voice is muffled and distant. "*Eight minutes. You guys have eight minutes to find the sequence.*"

"We'll show this to him later," you say. "For now we need the *second* step in the sequence, not the sixth."

You've found a special code! Be sure to write it down.

Check the Kitchen *ON PAGE 57*
Inspect the Sleeping Quarters *ON PAGE 68*
Hurry to the Supply Closet *ON PAGE 70*

150

The Physics Lab looks like something out of a college lecture hall: there are four rectangular tables with those chemical-resistance black tops, with lasers pointing at targets with computers connected at either end. A giant dry erase board stands at the front of the room covered in formulas and notes. The ceiling is exposed, with ductwork and pipes and wires. On the ground, there are stacks of printed paper *everywhere*.

"This is a lot of data," Penny says. She tries to lift a stack of paper up to her knees but fails.

"It's the printed code for the particle accelerator algorithm," Jay explains. "We have the Physics interns go through it line by line, checking for bugs. It's not always necessary, but it keeps them busy!"

You clear your throat, and Jay remembers you're an intern. "It's a good learning experience, of course," he says.

"Of course," you say skeptically.

To change the subject, Jay points across the room to the main table by the dry erase board. "Ah-ha! There she is. The CS Rifle."

He holds the Causality Smoother Rifle up for you to examine. It's small enough to fit in a backpack, and the barrel is short and stunted. The grip is curved strangely, but seems to fit Jay's hand just right. Altogether, the CS Rifle looks like the lowercase letter 'd' on its side.

"How's it work?" you ask.

"Just like any gun: point and shoot." Without warning, he points it at the dry erase board and fires. The noise is tolerable, a low *pfft* sound, and a thick beam of light shoots across the room. It strikes the board and disappears.

"Nothing happened," you say.

"Uh huh. Nothing was *supposed* to happen, young Mister Heller," Jay says. "It only works on atoms in the wrong place in time. The dry erase board belongs here, so it stays here." He holds it out to you.

You take it, feeling its weight. "So I could shoot you and nothing would happen?"

Jay gives a nervous laugh. "Yes, *theoretically*, but let's not go testing that hypothesis today, okay?"

Penny asks, "How did those atoms get stuck in time anyways?"

Jay's expression becomes serious. "That's a good question. Let's return to the Control Room and discuss what happened during the test."

Find out what Jay means *ON PAGE 22*

You click on the word SHREWD. A new line appears, then another, tapping out one letter at a time:

```
        INCORRECT INPUT
  CORRECT CHARACTER MATCH: 4
SYSTEM LOCKDOWN IN: ONE ATTEMPT
```

"Dang it," you say.

"But look, it has four characters in common!" Penny elbows you. "Come on, don't give up so easily. We can definitely get it with four out of six right."

"Okay, okay."

The screen now shows three options:

BEHEAD   THREAD   RACKET

Which is it? This is your last attempt!

To guess **BEHEAD**, *GO TO PAGE 78*
To guess **THREAD**, *HEAD TO PAGE 33*
To guess **PACKET**, *OPEN PAGE 116*

152

You remain frozen in place, CS Rifle held across your belly. The Causality Neutrino pulses with energy behind you, almost like a lighthouse, except you've never seen a lighthouse that makes such a strange humming sound.

A crackle of electricity shoots across the room, striking one of the tables in front of you. Its atoms turn bright white, spreading apart and disappearing into the air and ground like mist.

You desperately want to turn around. Knowing the orb is behind you and not being able to see is torture. Your willpower is waning!

You're about to turn your head when abruptly there's a popping noise, and the light in the room dims.

Jay immediately slumps his shoulders in relief. "That was close. *Real* close. You did very well, young mister Heller!"

"So the Causality Neutrino is still running wild?" you ask. "I thought it ended with the large loop test.

Jay shakes his head as he leads you back into the Control Room. "Unfortunately not. But we will discuss that later. Now that we have the CS Rifle, let's go get Penny."

Turn your attention to Penny *ON PAGE 29*

SNEAK PEEK

Welcome to the Middle of Nowhere!

You are TYLER PAULSEN, rookie hiker, camper, and all-around nice guy. In fact, this happens to be your first camping trip ever. You might even be enjoying yourself... that is if you weren't alone, and so deep in the remote wilderness!

You've spent the better part of the day on this rocky, uncomfortable ridge, staring down into the snowy clearing below. So far, not much has happened. There have been no lights, no sounds... nothing but the constant crackle of your roaring fire. The heat feels good against your back as you crunch down on another bite of granola bar. If only you weren't so thoroughly bored.

The envelopes started arriving more than a year ago. Always blank and with no return address, they came stamped with strange postmarks from all over the world. At first they turned up intermittently and you brushed them off. Then they arrived once a month, until finally, several times each week.

The contents were always the same: a single piece of odd vellum paper. On each, the same set of coordinates, the same date, and two bold words:

COME ALONE

Well that date is finally today. And right now? The GPS on your phone tells you you're staring down at the exact spot of those coordinates.

I hope this isn't a joke, you think to yourself. The very thought forces you to look around for maybe the hundredth time. But as you scan the tree-line, it occurs to you that you really have no enemies. And your friends? Well to be honest, none of them are interesting enough to actually pull something like this off.

Besides, watching you sit uneventfully on some cold mountain ridge would be a pretty boring payoff. Especially for such a long con.

No, there has to be a reason for all this. Something important. Something someone went through a tremendous amount of trouble for.

154

Suddenly you feel something. A vibration at first, then a rumble. Your teeth chatter together as the ground begins trembling violently beneath you. The tremors go on for a long moment, driving you from nervous to uncomfortable to outright frightened.

You drop to one knee, reaching for something to steady yourself. Then, just as suddenly as it started, everything comes to an abrupt halt. When you look up again you have the odd sensation that you're still moving, but you soon realize it's only the trees continuing to sway from the aftershock.

An earthquake?

You've never been through one before. You have nothing to compare it to, really. Nothing to say whether–

Your mouth drops open. Down below, the clearing is no longer empty. Impossibly, where there was nothing only moments ago? A gigantic, reaching wall of stone stands before you.

It's tremendous. Ugly. The base of it disappears somewhere in the valley below your campsite. The top is flung high into the mountain mist, lost to the sky.

It's more of a tower, you realize, than a wall. The structure has a definite shape and form to it, but in many places it also doesn't. You find yourself wondering who would design such a thing, and why. But those questions pale in comparison to the even bigger mystery:

How in the world did it get here?

You glance down at your watch. It's nearly dusk. The tower – or whatever it is – stands silhouetted against the dying light. You blink a few times and rub your eyes. Nothing changes. It's still there.

Your foot takes a step forward on its own. The movement is alarming but at the same time it makes you want to laugh. An enormous, hideous-looking tower just erupted into existence seemingly from out of nowhere. And you're actually thinking of checking it out?

As if in answer, the ground rumbles again. Just an aftershock, you think. Or maybe something else... An invitation?

The sky seems to darken with every passing second. You pull out the latest envelope and stare down at the paper. The writing hasn't changed. It says the same thing as always.

This is the day.

This is the time.

This is the place.

If you're going to explore the tower, you'd better get moving.

The hill is steep. Carefully you pick your way downward, crunching through the thin layer of snow while trying to maintain even footing. As you get lower, the tower seems to loom even taller before you. The sheer enormity of it is intimidating.

This is too dangerous, you think to yourself. You should turn back. But then you think about all the letters, and all the waiting. All the trouble you took to backpack your way out here, and all the time you spent sitting around, staring at the clearing.

Besides, the tower invited you. Or more accurately, someone inside the tower likely did. How could it be dangerous after sending all those letters? That makes sense, right?

Sure it does.

Up ahead, the ground levels out. As you get closer to the structure, you notice a strange mist has formed near the base. It's all grey, and thick, and more than a little foreboding. As you stare into it, it seems to roll and churn with a life of its own.

"Hello?" you call out. Your voice is all but swallowed by the mist. "HELLO?"

Silence answers. You open your mouth to call again, but suddenly feel silly. Maybe if you got a little closer someone would hear you. You're still a long distance away, maybe as much as half a mile. With all the fog it's hard to tell.

I should probably go back and get my things, you think. In your rush down the hillside, you forgot to bring anything with you. No food, no water, not even your utility knife. You feel a little foolish.

As you turn around however, a shudder runs through you. The swirling grey mist has closed in behind you. It envelops you now, blocking your exit. Surrounding you in every direction.

Every direction except straight ahead...

156

You walk slowly, allowing the mist to prod you gently toward the jagged tower. It's getting colder, darker. You miss your campsite, and especially, your fire.

I'm invited, you keep telling yourself. The words are meant to console you, but for some reason you still doubt them. *I was told to come here.* You glance up at the gargantuan stone megalith, looking for answers. It stares impassively down at you, neither menacing nor welcoming.

All around you the air is still, silent. You're standing squarely in the shadow of the tower now. Up ahead, the mist parts in two possible directions. To the left you see a small clearing – an opening in the fog. On your right you see the edge of a forest, preceded by a twisted, gnarled tree. Both ways still lead forward, in the direction you have to go. Okay, it's time to choose!

Which way will you go when you explore...

THE
TOWER
OF
NEVER THERE

ABOUT THE AUTHORS

David Kristoph lives in Virginia with his wonderful wife and two not-quite German Shepherds. He's a fantastic reader, great videogamer, good chess player, average cyclist, and mediocre runner. He's also a member of the Planetary Society, patron of StarTalk Radio, amateur astronomer and general space enthusiast. He writes mostly Science Fiction and Fantasy. www.DavidKristoph.com

Danny McAleese started writing fantasy fiction during the golden age of Dungeons & Dragons, way back in the heady, adventure-filled days of the 1980's. His short stories, The Exit, and Momentum, made him the Grand Prize winner of Blizzard Entertainment's 2011 Global Fiction Writing contest.

He currently lives in NY, along with his wife, four children, three dogs, and a whole lot of chaos. www.dannymcaleese.com

NOTES

Printed in Great Britain
by Amazon